break any woman down

winner of the flannery o'connor award for short fiction

break any woman down

stories by dana johnson

the university of georgia press · athens and london

Published by the University of Georgia Press
Athens, Georgia 30602
© 2001 by Dana Johnson
Set in 10 on 14.5 Electra
Printed and bound by Maple-Vail
The paper in this book meets the guidelines for
permanence and durability of the Committee on
Production Guidelines for Book Longevity of the
Council on Library Resources.

Printed in the United States of America
05 04 03 02 01 C 5 4 3 2 1

Library of Congress Cataloging-in-Publication Data
Johnson, Dana, 1967–
Break any woman down : stories / by Dana Johnson.
p. cm.
"Winner of the Flannery O'Connor award for short fiction."
ISBN 0-8203-2315-2 (alk. paper)
1. United States—Social life and customs—20th century—
Fiction. I. Title.
PS3610.O33 B74 2001
813'.6—dc21   2001027723

British Library Cataloging-in-Publication Data available

for Sim Sadler

contents

melvin in the sixth grade

Maybe it was around the time that the Crips sliced up my brother's arm for refusing to join their gang. Or it could have been around the time that the Crips *and* the Bloods shot up the neighborhood one Halloween so we couldn't go trick-or-treating. It could have even been the time that my brother's friend, Anthony, got shot for being at the wrong place at the wrong time. But my father decided it was time to take advantage of a veteran's loan, get out of L.A., and move to the suburbs. Even if I can't quite nail the events that spurred the move, I know that one and a half months after I climbed into my father's rusted-out Buick Wildcat and said good-bye to 80th Street and hello to Vermillion Street with its lawns and streets without sidewalks, I fell for my first man.

From the day Mrs. Campbell introduced him to the class, reprimanded us for laughing at his name, and sat him down next to me, I was struck by Melvin Bukeford with his stiff jeans, white creases ironed down the middle, huge bell-bottoms that rang, the kids claimed, every time the bells knocked against each other. Shiny jeans because he *starched* them. Melvin sporting a crew cut in 1981 when everybody else had long scraggly hair like the guys in Judas Priest or Journey. Pointed ears that stuck out like Halloween fake ones. The way he dragged out every single last word on account of being from Oklahoma. The long pointed nose and the freckles splattered all over his permanently pink face. Taller than everybody else because he was thirteen.

All that and a new kid is why nobody liked him. Plus he had to be named Melvin. All us kids, we'd never seen anything like him before, not in school, not for real, not in California. And for me he was even more of a wonder because I was just getting used to the white folks in West Covina, the way they spoke, the clothes they wore. Melvin was even weirder to me than the rest of them. It was almost like he wasn't white. He was an alien of some kind. My beautiful alien from Planet Cowboy.

I was writing *Melvin Melvin Melvin Melvin, Mrs. Avery Arlington Bukeford* on my Pee Chee folder by Melvin's second week of school. We walked the same way home every single school day. I fell in love with the drawl of his voice, the way he forgot the "e" in Avery; "Av'ry," he said it soft, or "AV'ry" when he thought I'd said the funniest thing, squinting at me sideways and giving me that dimple in his left cheek. All that made me feel like, well, just like I wanted to kiss my pillow at night and call it Melvin. So I did. "Ohhh, Mellllvin," I said, making out with my pillow every night. "Ohhh yeahh, Melvin."

I was keeping all that a secret until my eighteen-year-old brother saw my folder one day and asked me who Melvin was. "None ya," I said, and he said he knew it had to be some crazy-looking white boy—or a Mexican, because that's all West Covina had.

"Avery's done gone white boy crazy!" he called out. "I'ma tell Daddy!"

I ran into my room and slammed the door to stare at my four bare walls because Daddy had made me take down the posters I'd had up, all centerfolds from *Teen Beat* and *Tiger Beat* magazines. For one glamorous week I had Andy Gibb, Shaun Cassidy, and Leif Garret looking down on me while I slept. But one day Daddy passed my door, took one look at Leif Garret all blonde and golden tan in his tight white jeans that showed off a *very* big bulge, and asked me, "Avery, who in the *hell* are all these white boys?"

"Oh, Daddy, that's just Andy—"

"Get that shit down off those walls right now," Daddy said. He glared at Leif Garret.

I couldn't figure out why he was yelling at me. "But why—"

"What did I say?" he demanded.

"Take the posters down," I mumbled. And that's why I was staring at four blank walls.

But that was OK, because Melvin was my world. I didn't need him up on the wall. I had him in my head. I turned on the radio to listen to Ozzy Osbourne, who'd just bitten the head off a dove a few days before, singing about going off the rails on a crazy train.

Two months since being the new girl myself, Melvin was the only one who called me by my name; otherwise the other kids usually named me after my hairstyle. Like Minnie Mouse or Cocoa Puffs if I wore my hair in Afro puffs. Or Afro Sheen if my mother had greased my hair and pressed it into submission the night before. Or Electric Socket if I was wearing a plain old Afro. Avery. To hear that coming out of someone else's mouth at school was like hearing "Hey, Superstar."

They were warming up to me, though. Lisa White, who always smelled like pee, had invited me to her Disneyland party. Why, I don't know, but I was going, grateful to be going. For no reason, one day, she said, "Hey, you," when she saw me standing by the monkey bars watching her and a bunch of friends jumping rope. "Come to my party if you want to." What I heard was something like, "Hey you, you just won a trillion, bizillion, cabillion dollars."

But everything had become even more tricky than usual. Lisa didn't like Melvin. Nobody did.

One day when the smog wasn't so bad in the San Gabriel Valley (the air was only orange, not brown, and you could sort of see the mountains if you squeezed your eyes some), Melvin and I stopped at the same place we did every day after school: by the ivy in front of Loretta Morales's house on the corner, fat Loretta with feathered hair and green eyes, in high school now, even though we used to play Barbies together, who got down with boys now, who had a mother in a wheelchair for no reason I could figure out. She could walk, Mrs. Morales.

Melvin stuck his hand in the ivy, pulling at this and that, not finding what he was looking for. "Hmm," he said. "Av'ry girl, I b'lieve you done took my cigarettes for yourself, ain't you?"

"Nuh uh!" I grinned at him and hugged my folders and books to my chest. "You just ain't looking good."

"Well, then, help me out some." He brushed his hands through the ivy like he was running them through bathwater to test it.

"There's rats in there." I wasn't going to put my hands in the ivy because it was dark and I couldn't see. If I couldn't see, there was no need to just stick my hands into all that dark space like a crazy person, I didn't think.

Melvin took off his jean jacket and handed it to me. It had MEL spelled out on the back with silver studs you pressed into the fabric. He was getting serious about looking for those Winstons. I put my face in his jacket and smelled it, since he wasn't watching me. It smelled like smoke and sweat and general boy. From then on forever, I decided, I would love the smell of boy.

"Here we go," he said in a minute. He stood up, tapped the package on his palm, pulled out the cigarette, popped it in his mouth, took the match that always seemed to be tucked behind his ear, struck it on his boot, and cupped the match while he lit his smoke, so the fire wouldn't go out. He drew a deep suck on his cigarette and then threw his head back and blew the smoke up toward the sky. Then he rolled the packet of cigarettes in the sleeve of his white T-shirt. I watched all this like a miracle.

"I been dying for that cigarette all day long. You don't know," he said, letting it dangle between his lips. He winked at me. "Whoo weee!" he hollered.

But I did know. How it felt to want something so bad. Whoo weee, Melvin. How could *you* not know?

Melvin tried to take his jacket back. "I got it," I said.

He shrugged. "If you wont to."

But five steps later we were at my street. Verdugo. So I had to give the jacket back anyway.

"Hey, Melvin," I started, trying to kill time and keep him with me a little longer, "you going to Lisa White's Disneyland party?" But the second the words were out of my mouth, I knew it was the dumbest question I could have asked. Like Lisa would have asked Melvin to her party, like Lisa even *thought* about Melvin. That was just stupid to even think. How dumb *are* you? I asked myself.

Melvin took his cigarette out of his mouth and offered me a puff, he knew I wouldn't. We had that little joke going on between us. He got a kick out of me being a Goody Two-shoes and not taking a puff, even though I nearly died at the thought of my lips touching something that Melvin's lips touched. He grinned. "There's your brother," he said, trying to scare me about the cigarette, but I knew Owen was already at work.

"You ain't funny, Melvin Bukeford," I said, and punched him in the shoulder.

He rubbed it like it hurt. I guess I punched him harder than I thought. "Dang, Killer, you tough when you wont to be, ain't you?" He took another puff before he said, "Lisa ast me to go to her party, but I said I didn't b'lieve I could cause of the money, but shoot, I can steal me enough money to go to Disneyland, I just ain't too impressed with her or no Disneyland neither."

I could not believe what I was hearing. Lisa asked Melvin *and* he said no? I thought I was asked because I was liked—or on my way to be liked.

Melvin said, "She just askin everybody to say that everybody came to her little party. So what about her little pissy party." He stubbed out his cigarette. "Later, Miss Av'ry," he said, pulling on his jacket. "And don't be reaching into my stash of cigs else a big rat'll chew off your fingers."

"Nuh uh, Melvin!" I sang. I still stung from Lisa not really warming up to me that much after all, but Melvin's teasing and winking and dimples and smoke drifting hazy over his watery blue eyes made me happier. I would never need anything else in a man as long as I walked the planet earth. I watched him walk downhill in that odd slopey way he did, knees bending a little too deep at every step, like a flamingo. A flamingo smoking a cigarette wearing a studded denim jacket.

By the time I was walking through the door, home from school, Mama was running out the door to catch the bus to her first job at the sprinkler factory and later, her room-cleaning job, like always. I was only eleven but already taller than she was—and bigger all the way around. She was a little woman with a tiny neat Afro, but you didn't mess around and confuse the little and the tiny with the way she ran things. And with Daddy, when you saw big and tall, you didn't mess around with that either.

She didn't wait for me to speak before she started telling me what all I had to do. ". . . And the dishes, and put that pot of beans on. I already seasoned them. Don't put no more salt in them beans and mess em up, do and you know what you gone be in for. And your Aunt Rochelle sent you some more clothes. They in the living room. Be sweet." She patted me on the shoulders, hard, heavy so you could hear it even. Then she was out the door.

I was afraid to even look in the living room to see what kind of clothes were waiting for me. Aunt Rochelle's hand-me-downs from somebody's friend's cousin's daughter, used to be cool, but now that I was living in this new house in this new city far enough from L.A. that we were grateful when we saw other black people around town, I didn't like the hand-me-downs so much anymore because they were one more thing the kids could pick on me about. The fancy pants were Dittos or Chemin de Fers or Sergio Valentes or jackets that were Members Only. When they weren't calling me Afro Sheen they were calling me Polyester or Kmart, where I got my good clothes. Or they called me Welfare for getting in the "county" line when I lined up for my lunch from the free lunch program for people who needed it.

When I told my mother and father that I wanted different clothes, my mother said, "Chemin de Who for how much? You must be out your mind."

And of course I was. All eleven-year-olds were. I was out of my mind, especially for Melvin. Couldn't anybody understand that if I had just one cool outfit, like Melvin, I'd be on my way to the kids liking me for reals? Cool outfits may not have worked for Melvin, but he was an alien. I wasn't. If I tried hard enough, I'd be *in*. I found these lime-green polyester slacks that I really liked and put the rest of the clothes in the bottom of my bedroom closet. I imagined him saying, "Whoo wee, Av'ry! Check you out!"

Melvin was going to get his ass kicked after school. I heard it from Terri Stovendorf, the tomboy with the protruding forehead and sharp teeth on the side like a dog. She got drunk behind the portables, cheap mobile add-ons to the rest of the elementary school. She was always pushing me around, making fun of the way I spoke. I didn't know there was anything wrong with the way I spoke. I said "prolly" when it was "probably." I said "fort" when they said "fart." I said I was "finna" go home and not "getting ready" to go home. That's how we'd always spoken and it was good enough until the suburbs. I started studying the kids and editing myself. *Mama*, I practiced in the mirror at home. *I'm go-eng to do my homework. Go-eng. Who farted? Somebody farted?*

"Groovy Jan and Cindy and Bobby and Marcia," Owen said, whenever he heard me. "Grue-vee."

When Terri told me the news, I was at the water fountain at recess taking a break from tetherball, trying to get some water from the warm trickle coming out. I had to put my lips right up against the spout and tried not to look at the gum somebody had stuck down by the drain. When I picked my head up and wiped the water from my mouth, Terri called me. "Hey, Burnt Toast."

I turned around.

"Nice pants."

"Really? Thanks." I smiled at her shyly.

"I was kidding, dumb-ass."

I scratched my scalp because I didn't know what else to do. I had eight neat cornrows that ran from my hairline to the base of my neck.

"Listen," Terri said, suddenly doing business. "You and that country cowboy guy are always going around." We said "going around" to mean dating. I smiled at the thought that people thought Melvin and I were together, even though I was still trying to keep my distance from him in front of other people. I was scared of having more wrath heaped on me.

"What are you smiling at, stupid?"

"We're not going together," I mumbled. I started kicking around a rock with my imitation Vans, which were cooler than cool sneakers. Mine were knockoffs from Kmart.

"No duh," Terri said. "Like Country Cowboy would even go around with a nigger. I meant, like, walking around and stuff."

I had been called so many names that even "nigger" didn't faze me anymore. Not so much anymore. There were Mexicans and Philippinos and Chinese kids sprinkled throughout the class, but they blended better than me. There was more than one of each of them, and when they were called "taco" when they were from Portugal or "chink," even when they happened to be Philippino or Korean, that was the best kids like Terri could do with them. With me, there seemed to be endless creativity. So all I said to Terri was "Melvin and me don't go around, walk around together. His house is on *my* way home."

"Whatever. He's going to get his ass kicked after school today, and you better not tell him."

"Why?"

"Because I'll kick your ass, too."

"No, I mean . . ." I started cracking my knuckles. A bad habit I still have. I finally left the rock alone. "I mean, why are y'all going to beat up Melvin?"

Terri looked at me with disgust and wonder, like I was eating my own boogers, like Casey McLaughlin did. He modeled kid underwear because he was good looking; long eyelashes like a deer, and lips that always looked like there was lipstick on them. You could see him in those color junk ads that were always shoved in every mailbox in the neighborhoods, and he was as stupid as a stick.

"Are you a total moron?" Terri ran her hands through her stringy brown hair and left before I could answer.

I went looking for Melvin to tell, but I couldn't be *seen* telling him. I saw him sitting on a swing, all alone. Spinning in one direction real fast to tighten the swing chains and then spinning the other way as fast as he could to get that dizzy rush. The playground was full: a bunch of kids were playing touch football in the field, all the tetherballs were taken, two dodgeball games were going on, and both of the handball courts were taken. I couldn't see Terri, or cross-eyed Eddie Chambers, or nasty Hector Hernandez, who was always grabbing himself and lapping his tongue in and out like a snake at the girls. They would all be the ringleaders after school. The coast seemed clear enough to warn Melvin, but before I could make my way over to him, somebody called me.

"Hey, Turd Head," Harry Collins called out to me, my name whenever I wore cornrows. "We need one more person for butt ball." He walked over toward me with the red rubber ball while I tried to figure out how to say no. Butt ball hurt. You and one other person had to volunteer to get on your hands and knees facing the handball wall while two people threw the ball at you and tried to nail you in the behind. It hurt, for one, and for another, I never seemed to get my chance to try to nail somebody in the behind. Plus, that day there were my lime-green pants to think about. I didn't want to get dirt smudges on them. "Well?" Harry bounced the ball as though each bounce was a second ticking away. I stared at his stomach, which was always, no matter what, poking out from a shirt that was too small for him.

"I don't want to, Harry."

"Tough titty. We need another person."

"Well, I don't want to get my pants dirty." I kept looking over at Melvin to make sure he was still on the swings across the playground. If recess ended before I got a chance to tell him, he wouldn't have a warning.

"C'mon, man," Harry said. "Quit wasting time." He grabbed the front of my 94.7 KMET T-shirt that I'd gotten from somewhere and wore in hopes I'd have at least one cool piece of clothing. It was one of the radio stations that played Def Leppard and AC/DC, though in secret I still liked my Chi Lites 45, "Have You Seen Her?" better. Harry started pulling me toward the handball court, and when I resisted, he pulled so hard I fell down. I looked over at the swings. Melvin wasn't there. My slacks had a tear where I fell on my knees.

I got mad because I told him to leave me alone and he didn't. I started to cry because I was mad and couldn't kick Harry's ass, couldn't do anything.

"You all right, Av'ry?" Melvin drawled, and suddenly he was standing beside me. I was happy he was there and scared to talk to him, to be caught with Melvin, be a combo with Melvin, permanently paired so nobody would ever accept me because of my connection to Country Cowboy. But I was still in love with his pointy costume ears, and when he spoke my name, it was the first time I'd heard it all day. Not even our teacher, old powdery Mrs. Campbell, had called on me that day. So I mumbled a thanks, I'm OK, and Harry sneered at the both of us just when the freeze bell rang.

It was the bell that told us recess was over and we were to stop whatever it was we were doing, whatever games we were playing, and come back inside. We always took the bell literally. Until the bell stopped ringing, we froze right on the spot, like statues, like mannequins. There were me, Harry, and Melvin, frozen, along with everybody else on the playground, while tetherballs kept twirling and balls kept bouncing.

This is how kids start fights: "Hey, so and so. I'ma kick your ass." For no reason, out of the blue. So when Melvin was trying to leave school with his jean jacket slung over his shoulder, that's what cross-eyed Eddie said to him. Everybody else just agreed. I had warned Melvin, but all he did was frown and offer me half his piece of Juicy Fruit.

There was, then, the usually core group of fighters and the spectators when Eddie shoved Melvin. "C'mon, Country Cowboy. Fuckin Elvis." Eddie wasn't as tall as Melvin, but he was big and sloppy. Melvin didn't seem concerned, though. He ran his right hand over his crew cut and took his jacket off his shoulder. Melvin didn't want it to get dirty. He handed it to the person closest to him without thinking, gapped-tooth John Thompson, who said, "I'm not holding your stupid jacket, Country Ass," and dropped it on the ground. Just for that instant, Melvin looked dumb and awkward, as though he honestly didn't expect such rudeness from anybody. He picked up his jacket and dusted it off. I was behind him and panicked when I thought he might know this, turn around, and ask me to hold his jacket while he fought. What would I do? It had taken me weeks to get to where I was, which wasn't very far, but I was grateful for that slight break in the torture. The tiny thaw in the frost. I was going to Disneyland with Lisa White, and even if she didn't like me so much now, maybe at the party she would see who I really was and then like me.

"Av'ry, hold my jacket, will you?" Melvin held it out and his nostrils flared a little bit when I hesitated. I glanced at Terri, who was looking straight at me with a psychotic grin on her face. Melvin thrust the jacket at me. I took it. And then, well, it slipped from my fingers and fell to the ground. Melvin looked at his jacket and then at me, those pale blue eyes looking at me brand new and different from any time before. We both left the jacket there, and then he beat the shit out of Harry, then Hector, then Eddie. Not Terri, because she was a girl, but she chased me home for two weeks straight, even though I didn't hold the jacket, and even though Melvin didn't care when I told him that they were going to kick his ass after school.

Walking home after the fight, Melvin didn't say more than five words to me. I can't even say that he walked home *with* me, because he was walking fast and I couldn't keep up. His legs were so long, and for every stride he took I had to take two. I was looking forward to him searching for his cigarettes in the ivy, but he said he wasn't going to go the way we usually went. He was going home another way. I couldn't blame him for being disappointed in me, I'd let him down after he'd come to my rescue during recess. But couldn't he understand that, really and truly, it wasn't a personal thing. Couldn't he understand that I could be completely in love with him, but just not want to make waves? And anyway, it wasn't like I *threw* the jacket down or anything. It slipped.

"But, Melvin," I said, trying to get him to go my way. "This is the quickest way to get home. Your house is straight ahead. Plus, what about your cigarettes? Aren't you dying for a cigarette?"

"Darlin . . ." He pulled a cigarette from his jacket pocket and put it behind his ear. "I can get by with what I got right here until later."

Darlin. I'd never heard that from him, calling me that before. I didn't like the way it felt, like a pat on the head. Not like when he said my name, which felt like a kiss.

"See ya round," Melvin said and turned, walking uphill. I watched him for as long as I could see him, and I still didn't know that he was never going to walk my way again, but I was thinking, *You probably should have picked up his jacket. Pro-ba-bly.*

Too late. Melvin got farther and farther away, MEL on the back of his jacket, shimmering like diamonds, like he was some superstar. And me, I was feeling as though I wished somebody fighting had slugged me, too.

I walked up the hill to my house and replayed Melvin's fight. Only in my mind, it wasn't Melvin's fight. It became my fight. I imagined I had on a bad outfit, windowpane pants and a leather jacket, new — not used — and a large, perfectly round Afro like the one Foxy Brown had when she pulled a gun from it and blew away some white man who was messing with her. Owen was obsessed with Pam Grier and her big breasts, and I was awed by her ability to whup ass. People who messed with Foxy were sorry, all right. Just when they thought she was all brown sugar in a halter top, she had a gun or a karate kick to set them straight.

Listen, I said. I was talking to myself. *All y'all mothafuckas better leave Melvin alone. That's right, I cussed. And I did say, muthafucka, not mo-ther fuck-er. It's the way I speak, dumb-asses, and unless you want your butt kicked, you best to leave me and my man alone. Who you calling a nigga?* I swung around and pointed a gun at the nearest palm tree. *That's what I thought.*

I kept replaying my and Melvin's fight. When I got in the house, I was surprised to see Owen at the refrigerator, home from work early, drinking milk from a carton.

"You not supposed to be doing that. Mama said."

"Mama said," he mimicked me. "You always got to do everything everybody say, goody-goody. Who were you talking to, anyway?"

I put my books down on the dining room table, round and glass. I didn't want to stop my daydream. Melvin was holding my hand. *Darlin, I guess you told them what side of the sidewalk they can spit on, didn't you?*

I went to the cabinet for a glass and poured myself a glass of milk dramatically, to show Owen how it was supposed to be done. He thumped me on the head.

"You still ain't told me who you was talking to all loud."

I drank my milk down in two gulps, washed my glass out then and there because Mama liked her kitchen kept neat, and then I picked up my books so I could go to my room and get out of my torn green pants. "Nobody. OK? I wasn't saying anything to anybody. I was just talking to myself."

"Trippin," he said, making his way to his room. He hardly seemed fazed by anything, not even moving to the suburbs.

"Hey," I said. "Owen."

"What?"

"Isn't it weird going to school with all these white people some-time? Don't it make you feel . . ." My voice trailed off. I was look-ing for the word. "Bad? *Doesn't* it make you feel bad?"

"What?" Owen rolled his eyes. "I'm graduating this year, Ave. I ain't stuttin these white folks." He went into his room and closed the door and soon I could hear Peabo Bryson blaring from his stereo, *I'm so into you, I don't know what I'm going to do.*

Stuttin, Owen said. Stuttin meant "studying." I repeated the word in my head. I'd heard that word my whole life from my grandmamas, Mama, Daddy, everybody. But when Owen said it then, "stuttin" sounded like a word he'd just made up. For the first time I really heard what the kids in school heard when I spoke. Owen sounded strange to me, from someplace else, using that word. Part of a lan-guage I knew but was already beginning to forget.

three ladies sipping tea
in a persian garden

This morning I woke up on my back and alone, because already, I *think* I've been through another man. A fight about something stupid ended in sex. And then me, alone on my back, listening to my front door close too loudly. So I decided to do something, wear something, that made me feel not like a woman who is sad because of a man. And I called Sharzad. "Get your ass over here," she said. "I'm tired of my friend being sad. We will make our own fun, darling." That was this morning. Now, I'm knocking on her door and she's opening it.

"Look at you, you queen bitch!" Sharzad screams, cradling my face in her tiny hands. "So lovely." She kisses both my cheeks and pulls me into her small apartment, locking the door behind me. My head is wrapped in vibrant red material, wrapped around and around my head like a tower, a few braids poking out from the sides and the back, my version of the wispy tendrils I see in fashion magazines.

Sharzad stands back to get a better look and slaps her thighs. "Aha! Ha Ha!" She covers her mouth, but the crinkles around her almond eyes tell me that she is not through with me.

"You look like a fucking African princess. Turn around." She spins me around easily, though I'm much bigger than she. "That looks really cool, you bitch. What are you up to? Wait until Nasim sees you. She's going to die. Maybe this will be something to make her smile bigger."

I smile the smile I can't help, the one that near closes my eyes and stretches the corners of my mouth as far as they'll go, and Sharzad pulls me into her cramped kitchen. "Sit." In Sharzad's small apartment, one wall is all windows, most of them today cranked open to let in the fresh air. She never pulls the blinds down in her apartment, so there is always plenty of light, even on days when there is no sun.

Along the edge of her table, against the wall, and all along the windowsill, she keeps flowers—some she's bought and some she's picked from the countless plants she tends to on her balcony—dozens of shapes and colors: yellows, reds, purples, oranges, and whites in bud vases, jelly jars, miscellaneous glasses from big to small. She sits down, too, and strokes a flower petal the shape of a clover and the color of a bruise, placed in a glass shaped like a boot. "This little bastard . . ." Her voice trails. "It won't last longer than a day once it's picked. So gorgeous." I touch it, too, and it reminds me of baby skin.

"Have some tea, baby?"

I nod and Sharzad roots around in her cabinets, finally setting out Persian candies. My eyes light up as I reach for two pieces of the nougat and pistachio candy on delicate hand-painted dishes.

"Don't eat all the *gaz*, you little piggy," Sharzad says, pleased that I'm so easy to please. When she pours the tea, we sit in a moment of silence and I wonder why my tea never turns out like hers. Do I use too many tea leaves? Too little water? Steep it too long or too short a time? I sip the tea through the sugar cube in my mouth, just like Sharzad and her sister Nasim taught me. The cube dissolves, perfect for thirty seconds or even a minute, before the granules are few, and then gone. I reach for a handful of the candy called *pesh-mek*, just like cotton candy but white and flat, not so insistently pretty and pink.

"How is your back, Sharzad?" I notice her moving about her kitchen slightly stiff.

"Oh God, this fucking back. Even if I really want to, I don't know how I'm going to have a goddamn baby with this back." For two years now, Sharzad has been trying to decide. Does she want a baby? Or doesn't she? Is she too old to try now? Her health is not so good. And now her back pains her. She turns down the corners of her mouth as if to say, Ah well, what do I do? I wonder if Sharzad will ever have that baby. Before her back was her neck; before that, her stomach. We all agree that her baby with her handsome husband will be a beautiful child, with Sharzad's enormous brown eyes and Sharzad's hair, thick and black and long like sheets of heavy satin ribbon. Even if it's a boy. We can see that baby. Sharzad, a baby on her hip, then, again, is the one thing I cannot see.

"If I'm going to do it, I better do it soon," she lisps, a sugar cube lodged between her front teeth.

"Anh," I flip a limp wrist her way. "You got time." But I'm not sure I believe it, and pretty sure I don't know what I'm talking about.

"You. You should get yourself a baby," Sharzad says. She claps her hands and laughs heartily when I give her the big eyes.

"Find me a man, any man, and maybe I'll make that part of the deal. You date me? *Seriously* date me? Bam! Here's a baby. Small price to pay."

"Wait. What happened to your man? Just three weeks you've been with this one. He was so gorgeous! So sweet."

"Sharzad," I say, shaking my head. "No. Yes, he was gorgeous, sometimes sweet, but no." The kind of guy I pick time and time again—or they pick me. A pretty package that, when opened, is empty, so empty that when you peer inside the package, ever so hopeful, eternally hopeful, the depth of the package, the darkness of that depth, keeps you staring in disbelief. Is this it? This can't be it. Whose joke is this? There's got to be something *inside*. "Sharzad, you'd sell me out for a pretty man with a nice ass?" I keep eating the candy sitting in front of me on the table.

"Honey. When you get to be my age . . ." She gathers her hair and begins twisting it to make a bun but lets it drop suddenly. "That's a nice little snack, a pretty man with a nice ass. With an OK ass, even."

"*Your* age."

"I know I'm not *so* ancient, darling. But I'm not twenty anymore," she says with a knowing grin.

Me, I am twenty-six years old.

We sit at the table for a moment with our thoughts. It's three o'clock and the sunlight shines into Sharzad's eyes. I see specks of gold. Lately I've taken to recording moments, and this is one for when I'm old: Sharzad sitting at her table, color all around her, gold in her eyes.

In the alley below, someone in a car honks the horn again and again, insistent.

"These assholes," she mutters, and squeezes past me, out the screen and onto the balcony to look down onto the alley below. "They make so much noise. Who the—"

I've come out too and let the door slam behind me. We both see a blonde woman, nearly bald, all her hair cut into bleached nubs. I scream like I haven't screamed in a good two years, the last time I was on a roller coaster. Sharzad clutches my arm and screams, too, when she realizes, finally, that Nasim has cut off all her silky, waist-length black hair.

"Ahhh!" The two of us are like insane women, as if someone has jumped out from bushes with a knife in his hand.

I stumble back into the house, overcome by a fit of laughter, and Sharzad falls into me, knocking me onto her couch. We clutch our stomachs and roll on each other in hysterics. I can't believe my eyes, and neither can Sharzad, so it takes five minutes of tears streaming down our cheeks and stomach cramps from laughing to finally calm us down.

"Oh!" Sharzad says, wiping away the eyeliner that has run with all the tears. "She has really fucked-up now."

"Wow," I say, sober. "Wow." And then I'm laughing in fits again. "Where is she? Why isn't she coming in?"

"I dunno." Sharzad gets up, holding the small of her back. She goes out onto the balcony and looks down on the alley. "She's not there," Sharzad calls. She marches in and goes straight to the phone, dials her sister's number. "You bitch! What did you do? What mess did you get yourself into that I'm going to have to get you out of?

Get your ass over here. Now." She laughs into the receiver before she slams the phone down so hard that it makes a crunching sound when it settles into the cradle.

"Wow," I say. "Wow." Then the two of us are stupid and laughing again.

Sharzad pulls a bottle of cheap red wine out of her kitchen cabinet, two glasses, and pours without asking if I want any. I'm done in four gulps, so she pours me another right away. That woman standing beside the Jeep didn't look anything like Nasim. Anything at all. She has disappeared. Just like that.

"Play some music, Sharzad. Billie Holiday."

"Very nice. Come on, baby. Let's go outside and stay for a while. Wait for that lunatic. You go. I'll be there."

I wait for Sharzad out on the balcony. Below and all around the alley is nothing but concrete and apartment windows facing us. A garbage truck comes by, drowning out Billie claiming that *You ain't gonna bother me, no more. Woke up this morning and found, I didn't care for you, no more. No how.* I admire two potted sunflowers lurking behind me against the wall, peeking over my shoulder.

"Hello, sweeties," I say in baby talk. I can't help but speak to them like people, because their faces are staring at me. "Sharzad!" I call out, "what are these purple things?" I finger a pot of bright purple petals on the ledge.

"What, baby?" And then Sharzad screams. A door slams. It's Nasim, so I come inside to stare some more, so I can believe my eyes.

"Jesus Christ," I say.

"Wahh," Nasim whines. "Wahhh." She puts four fingers in her mouth and chews dramatically while Sharzad pulls at nubs of her hair roughly, trying to arrange something that is not there.

"Well," Sharzad steps back and says finally above Billie. "You really fucked-up this time."

"Wahhh," Nasim answers.

"Yep," I agree.

"Fuck-a you," Nasim says, the accent part Persian, part Italian.

Sharzad's English is perfect, Nasim's is not, Nasim having arrived in the States much later than her sister, having spent years and years in Rome after fleeing Iran.

"I had to do this thing, you see. I wanted to slice my hair for da very very long time. Make a change. Get it out my seestym."

"Is it out?" I peer at her. "Jesus. I hope it's out."

Nasim gives me the middle finger, the nail dirty with paint from her studio. "My-a God. And you? What is that thing on your head?"

I shrug.

"*Ma-donna*," Nasim says, completely at a loss.

We sit at the kitchen table, and Sharzad raises the bottle of wine along with her eyebrow. Nasim frowns and shakes her head violently. "No. Tea." So Sharzad puts more water on the stove.

"What in the hell were you *thinking*?" Sharzad pleads over and over again. "*What*?"

"Really? Is that bad? It is only hair, no?" Nasim scratches her scalp furiously, as if loosening dandruff. Her face, usually dusky and hinting brown, has a green pallor. Her olive skin tone is literally olive, thanks to the freshly yellow hair. But she still has the same plump lips, tiny for such strong words that always fly from them, those sharp, golden brown eyes. True beauty is impossible to erase.

"Actually . . ." I begin. My voice is high and hopeful, like I'm flirting with a man.

"Don't you fuckeeng lie to me."

"OK." I pause, take a deep breath. "It's crazy, Nas. A nightmare I cannot escape."

"Thank you," she says. "That is good."

"Here's your tea, you idiot," her sister says. She sits at the table. Nasim points to my head, shivers like she's caught a chill, which makes us laugh all over again.

Six years ago, when I was twenty and Sharzad was thirty-five and Nasim was thirty-eight, I was with a man I loved, the first man I ever loved. I was a little girl, Sharzad says. It's four-thirty and the sky is an orangish purple, the sun going away, leaving me. "You are not a little girl, anymore," Sharzad is lecturing, when I complain about my latest man.

"Bye-bye, sun," I say, tuning out and changing the subject, just like an adolescent.

"No," Nasim says. "It is just on the other side. Tomorrow, it will be back."

We're out on the balcony, our legs spread and our skirts hiked up. We want to even our skin colors. My legs are a weak brown, splotchy with a yellow hue, far from the rich brown of my arms, burgundy just underneath. Sharzad and Nasim want to be browner and browner. Browner than me.

"You leetle monkey," Nasim says, comparing arms. "Give me."

But I admire their shapely legs, the girlish indentations behind Sharzad's dimpled knees, Nasim's smooth calves and shins, no souvenirs of clumsiness and boyish ways like my legs. I tell them that they are beautiful. Sharzad says, "Thanks, Rosalind darling."

Nasim says, "Oh, you. You know notheeng."

"What a sweet little baby you were, when I first saw you," Sharzad says, talking still about the first time I was in love. I'd met Sharzad and Nasim at an art walk in West L.A. where Nasim and I were showing work. I was following around a tattooed boy with a goatee. I was completely and forever-and-a-day in love.

"If I would have said 'boo' to you, you would have fainted," Sharzad says. I smile, because she's right, and I miss that girl who was afraid of the slightest boo, aware of very little of the world around her, inches and moments away from her face. I see Sharzad, too, who then used to wear her hair in a tangled bun, strands swirling about her eyes lined deeply in Cleopatra-style black liner. And the skirts! Barely past the *cosplus*, as they say in Farsi—or "poosie," as Nasim says in English. Nothing much has changed in Sharzad, save the slight bags under her eyes that I never noticed so much before.

"This ugly thing, a leetle baby?" Nasim strokes my cheek, her honey eyes pouring warmth over my face. "Ha! My-a ass!"

I was a little baby, Sharzad was falling in love with her husband, and Nasim was battling with interchangeable insane artists she was continually throwing out of her bungalow.

I ask Nasim about a particular man whose name I butcher because it's Persian.

"My-a God. What are you trying to do to me? My hair is not enough tragedy ford-a you today? You have to bring up that, that *ding?*"

Sharzad picks a daisy from a pot and puts it behind my ear.

"Wait." I unwrap my braids and run my fingers through them. "Better to see my flower without this." Sharzad picks another daisy and puts it behind my other ear, arrangement and more arrangement. "Thank you." I wink at her. She kisses me on the forehead. Staring at all the daisies, I think of *he loves me, he loves me not.* I take one flower from behind my ear and begin to pluck the petals.

"Hey." Sharzad yanks the flower from my hands. "Don't kill my pretty flower for that." She puts what's left of the flower back behind my ear.

"Give me that thing." Nasim takes my wrap and piles it onto her head like a mess. It won't stay, because she has no idea how to wrap it. She looks ridiculous.

"Honey, no." Sharzad sits on her sister's lap. She throws her arms around Nasim's neck and kisses her on the cheek. "Not even that saves you."

"Ah, get off me, you cow you." Nasim turns her head to avoid Sharzad's kisses, but Sharzad coos in Farsi. I take one of my daisies and put it behind Nasim's ear, the wrap long since fallen to the ground. "These flowers . . . Zeba had so many at her funeral," Nasim says. "She loved these stupid leetle flowers."

I only met Nasim's best friend, Zeba, a few times, and she has been dead for nearly three months. Kidney failure. Nasim is just now coming out of her sadness, Nasim who is nearly impossible when she's happy, untouchable in grief. Zeba was tall with thick wiry hair and blue eyes. She was shy and liked to sing. One song I heard her sing in English, the tune I remember, but what was that song exactly? Zeba was the only person, other than Nasim's sister, who saw and knew Nasim when she was a little girl. I'm going to ask Nasim about the song, but she says, "Did I tell you this thing about Zeba? This is so great." Nasim pats Sharzad's behind to tell her to get off her lap.

"More tea?" Sharzad offers. "More wine?" She's leaving because she doesn't like to talk about Zeba, doesn't want Nasim to get in a mood.

"Bring the bottle," I suggest.

"Piggy," Sharzad says, but goes to get what I want.

"The last time I saw Zeba, the night before he died—"

"*She!*" Sharzad corrects. "How long have you been here?"

"She. I go into her room and she is seeting up in bed like an angel. Up against the pillow, her hair coming down and around like this." Nasim makes corkscrews in the air with her fingers. "Her lips and eyes, everything like this," Nasim kisses the tips of her fingers and spreads them as if releasing tiny doves from the palm of her hand. "Perfect. I said to her, 'My-a God, Zeba. You are gorgeous. What is this? Then this fuckeeng man comes into the room, he work as nurse there, magnifico, puffing the pillows, this and that with the pillows, ask if she is OK. He had the eyes like to put you in a spell. When he left, I said, 'You whore! This is why you look like a beautiful angel. Yesterday, you could not be bothered with me. Now look at you. No matter how sick you are, a handsome man is a handsome man.' Zeba laugh with me that day. So nice, it was." Nasim's smile fades and she picks at her fingernails. "And then, the next day, she die."

I don't know what to say, so run my hand along her arm.

"Ah, sheet," Nasim says, taking my hand in hers. "Sharzad! Bring me a glass for da wine, too!"

Inside the house, Sharzad has put on Arabic music and she dances, spinning around. We look at her through the glass wall between us. I never understand any of the words, neither do Sharzad and Nasim, but we sing along anyway and we always dance.

"You donkey! Where is my wine?" Nasim grins and mimics her sister's beckoning hands. She jumps up and pulls me toward the screen door. "Let's go dance."

Lulul, luhul, luhul, a man sings, and we sing along in our fake Arabic, hands high above our heads, clapping. Farsi and Arabic sound the same to me, and once when I told Sharzad this, she said, "You goofball! And you have the nerve to tell me that 'Persian' is not

PC. Better to say Iranian!" Now she's demonstrating the more Persian way to dance. "Like this, Lovely!" Sharzad thrusts her hips at me and shimmies her breasts. But in five years I haven't learned to do what she shows me, I only halfway do it. Nasim takes my hand and leads me, her face concentrated in mock intensity. Debonair and suave, like a man in the movies doing a tango. She spins me out and pulls me back in, but I fall into her and knock her into the couch, giggling.

"Better to dance with a doggy on three legs than with you!" She slaps my thigh. We lie on the couch watching Sharzad, catcalling and whistling. She flashes us her breasts.

"Please," Nasim raises her hand in protest, so I jump up from the couch and flash her mine, too. "*Ma-donna.* I am the prisoner of prostitutes. Where is my fuckeeng wine?" She dances to the kitchen and pours it herself.

"Hey!" I say, encouraged by Nasim's insults, and wine. "Pencil test!"

"You idiot. They are the same as last."

"Mine, too," Sharzad says, still thrusting her hips.

"No, I've been doing exercises."

"Honey." Sharzad's dance has ended and she's searching for another tape. "What the hell kind of exercises you been doing?"

"All kinds. Look!"

I search for a pencil and take one that Sharzad has been using to hold up an avocado plant.

"You better put that back," Sharzad says.

"I will. Look." I lift up my T-shirt and bra, and put a pencil under my breast. It falls to the floor. Last time it didn't. Sharzad's and Nasim's didn't, either. The pencil stayed right under our breasts, trapped by the weight. "I'm younger than you," I had whined.

"They're still supposed to have life!" But now I am triumphant. "Look at that! See? See? What'd I tell you?"

"You *estupid*." Nasim picks up the pencil off the floor. She's grinning at me. "You were bending over. That's why it falls. Forget about it. They are on their way down. Buy pretty bras, have another glass of wine, and shut up."

Nasim is waving her cigarette around dangerously, just missing me, tapping the ashes onto the balcony's concrete floor. She and her sister are arguing about my future in Farsi. They have tried to teach me a few words here and there. But their words don't stick. I'm past the age of learning languages, too? They say something something and something, words and sentences that all have the lilt of questions. This all started when I said, again, this time to Nasim, that I was tired of pretty packages. "I hate him," I say, "I don't want him anymore."

"You are a liar," Nasim says. "You are angry just because he maybe get tired of you before you get tired of him. You stick with him a leetle longer, if you want. He is delicious. But if you do not want to stick with him, don't. Why you make everything so hard?"

"Even if he is not the marrying kind, even if he doesn't want me to be his wife? Stay for a while?"

"Good for him. He's smarter than you think. Why do you care to be married? You are too young. Everyone running around getting married, like train wrecks, like disaster."

"Hey." Sharzad balls her fists and shakes her four-year-old wedding ring at Nasim. Her husband Clifford is good to her, but his quiet ways contrast with Sharzad's vibrancy; she is like a sunburst and he is like a leather chair by the fireplace.

"You too," Nasim says to her sister. "But at least Clifford is not

Persian and treating you like a property. No, no, no Rosalind." Nasim wags a finger. "Milk him dry. Not of the money, but of the other thing, do you see. He is like the most beautiful piece of art I will never paint. Just take him off the wall and put up another when you are tired of the painting."

But what do I do, I wonder, when I feel as though I am the one being taken off the wall?

Sharzad, who talked like Nasim earlier, when the day was young, is contrary. "Lovely wants a real man, not a concubine."

"Wait. I think—I'm pretty sure—I want both. A little extra on the concubine?"

"Oh, shut up." Nasim is frustrated. "You don't know what. You don't know. Send that delicious thing to me and stop ke-rying."

"*Ke*-rying," Sharzad mimics.

"*Cry*-ing," Nasim says, and kicks Sharzad's shin.

"Ouch, you ugly monster."

Nasim worries about her sister's health—the back and the stomach and whatever else lies ahead. She does not think that Sharzad can carry another person inside her. Sharzad sits between Nasim's legs and rolls her head from side to side while Nasim massages her neck.

Nasim, she will never have children. She loves children. She stops them on the street and talks to them business-like, and in her eyes I bet they see a woman who loves them for being good and beautiful and sometimes evil. They take her hand, let her touch them, answer all of her questions with shy grins. And then, they are walking down the street with their mamas and daddies, Nasim going her way, they going theirs.

I like children some of the time, scary little creatures who make me fear them and long for them. Sharzad likes them like playing dress-up—taking off the clothes when she is tired of them. Women like us, Sharzad and me, of course we will be mothers someday, because women like us are always afraid we've missed the boat.

The sun is one hour down, and Sharzad has just watered all of her plants and flowers. We sit in the dark, not really wanting the light on, and rely on the street lamps in the alley below. This is the best time to be on Sharzad's balcony. Even better than the hours of sun. This time of night, early night, the flowers smell the sweetest, the perfume is the thickest, and the air sits on our shoulders like a comforting hand. Three wine bottles have been emptied, the candy is long gone, and the curry chicken and rice that Sharzad threw together in the snap of a finger we all ate like wolves. Nasim even threatened Sharzad with her fork when she tried to take it away before she was finished. We're back to tea. Sharzad insisted when I asked for more wine. "No, baby," she said. "Have more tea. It's better for your tummy to digest all the food you ate today." And that was the end of it, just like a bossy mama.

But now Nasim is being the mother and preaching about the new shoes Sharzad showed us proudly. They turned her five-foot-two frame into five feet and five inches. "Sharzad, you cannot walk around in these kinds of shoes anymore," Nasim insists. "You try to show your ass, you hurt your back to be some sexy bitch. It is not good."

"You do it all the time! I'm not going to go around looking like an old lady before my time. More to the left, Nasim." Sharzad moves her sister's hand farther down her shoulder blades.

"Yes. I do it all the time. But I am not trying to be somebody's mama. Don't tell me how to do rubs. I know how to do rubs."

"Yes." I try to stir up more entertainment. "To the man in the art supply store, the bartender at the Good Luck Bar—"

"Me! You leetle whore. You keep your fingers busy in everybody's pants!"

"Ow. Take it easy. You're going to paralyze me. Where are my pants and people to rub? That's what I want to know."

"Stay out of this. I'm talking to the prostitute. You. Stay with that husband. You. Stay with the piece of art. Everybody." Nasim says, "Get up, Sharzad. Everybody stay with their own disasters, yes?"

"Yesss, Sharzad. I have to go!" I say. Leaving her house is never easy. She never wants to let you go. I give her a big hug and lift her off the ground. I remember her back, so I put her down.

"One more cup of tea."

"Noooo."

"Awww."

"Oh, let the leetle monkey go," Nasim says, hugging me from behind. I turn around and she kisses both my cheeks and takes my hand. "I'm sick of her face. Get out, you."

"Oh, I almost forgot. Where's my headwrap?"

"God. That thing," Sharzad says, looking around. "Where is it?"

"There." Nasim lets go of my hand and goes out on the balcony. "Here." She throws it to me as she comes back inside.

"You sure you don't want this for your, um . . ." I search for a word. "Hair?"

Nasim slaps her bicep and raises her forearm sharply, fist closed. The Italian salute. No. She doesn't want it. I wrap it around my neck like a scarf.

Sharzad hugs me three more times before I leave, Nasim insults me one more time before I leave, and I say, "Good-bye, sweetie," to the sunflower, tall as a man, just to my right as I make my way to the door. It's late dark now. Maybe six? Maybe seven? Soon,

Sharzad's husband will come home to her, Nasim will go home to whomever she allows to be there. Me, I guess I'll do the same.

When I make my way downstairs, I look up at the balcony.

"Good-bye, lovely. Good-bye, you very bad girl," Sharzad and Nasim call out, their arms around each other, free hands waving.

"Be nice to the boys, darling." "No! Only if they deserve it and are nice to her!" And then, I am walking down the alley, farther and farther away from them, no more voices in the dark.

As I walk I remember a moment earlier in the day when the sun had not quite left our side of the world and Sharzad was painting my toes and Nasim was telling me that I should wear eyeliner to bring out my brown eyes, and there was this thing, a feeling like a voice, a nagging voice, trying to tell me something, maybe trying to tell me a way to *be*. It felt like being so happy and so sad. I couldn't name it. Almost, though. Almost.

I was so close to getting it, like that song of Zeba's I can almost remember. The melody, I have, but the missing words to the lyrics, I don't have.

They're just on the tip of my tongue.

break any woman down

Bobby used to love to watch himself so much, videos of his work. He called himself "shy," just like all his other actor friends. Get those people in a room, though, and you've never seen so much goddamn ham in your life. With Bobby it was always rewind, back up, what did you think of that shot? I look pretty good, right? Bobby had eyes like caramel, shiny, honey brown, clear with dark brown rings around the pupil. Hair black like ink with waves that made you want to rub your lips in them. A strong chin you wanted to rub your cheek against.

Watching Bobby's work with him, it was always, "My nose cool, do you think? What about my ass? Kinda pale, huh?" You wouldn't think somebody so pretty'd have to be told it every damn day of his life. But that was Bobby. And don't expect him to say "thank you" after you told him he was fine. He knew he was fine. Just needed that echo from somebody else. Me, usually.

I'm thinking about the OK times. Not the good times, but the OK times, after Bobby made me stop stripping and I was beginning to hate him but didn't know it. His career was doing fine—he'd just finished this little thing for the Playboy Channel and he was happy but trying not to show it. He was also proud of a couple of low-budget movies he had just gotten copies of in the mail, and that's what we were watching one night, one of the last good nights. In the video we were watching, Bobby was a grocery boy in the old days, the 1800s or something, delivering bread to this blonde bitch with her hair in a bun. I was teasing him about the knickers and hat he was wearing.

"Shhh," he said.

In the movie, Bobby stepped through the door with a sack full of groceries, mostly fruit. A bunch of bananas, zucchini. Real corny. Nice lighting, though. Warm.

Miss Hazelton? I'm delivering the goods you requested.

Delivery boy. Come in. I have some odds and ends I need you to take care of.

And then Bobby was getting his dick sucked.

I don't know. To me, it seemed like something was missing. Like the scene had progressed too fast or something? I mean, fast even for porno. I had started watching a lot of it with Bobby, so I was getting real good at telling the bad ones from the good. We wanted Bobby's work to be good, so we rehearsed Bobby's lines over and over, trying to figure out how he should play the scene. Shy, like he was afraid of the lady? Or slick, like he was in charge and knew he was going to get some. Somehow though, he wasn't looking like either one in the scene. He was looking like a guy in a jacked-up outfit saying lines. When I told Bobby this, that something was missing, he said, "Shhh," and asked if his back looked cut enough, and maybe he'd have to spend more time working his back at the gym.

But it was perfect. Smooth, a few freckles here and there. Nice and tan. Actually, kind of fake tan, because he went to this tanning salon to stay brown all year, even though you didn't really need all that in Los Angeles. Extra brown, because he had a little hue to him since he was Greek, distant family from Corfu Island. Bobby was just from Brooklyn, though. And damn if I didn't have to hear about Brooklyn every day of my life. If he wasn't playing out Corfu, then I had to suffer through Brooklyn. Take your ass back and leave California to the rest of us then, I wanted to say, but never did. Bobby claimed he couldn't leave because he wanted to act, but that boy didn't want to act. He just wanted to get looked at while he was trying to act.

So that night, watching Bobby trying to act, that was one of our OK nights. We lay in the middle of Bobby's studio apartment, on a futon mattress, our bellies tight with wine and angel hair pasta that Bobby had made just for me because I love it so much. And the both of us watched Bobby get worked on by the blonde, who was finally about to make him come, how I don't know, because she really wasn't doing it the way Bobby liked. She sucked it like she was afraid of it, not like she owned it.

Bobby always wanted to fast-forward the parts where he came, because he was embarrassed by the faces he made. But this I never, ever told him because I knew he'd ruin it for me, start acting it. In the faces he made, I could see him turn from what he thought he was. From Mr. Man with the world's biggest dick and all the power in the world to the little boy folded up on his mama's lap. Needy. That was the only time, for sure, I could see that he wasn't playing like he was working the camera, on an audition. The faces he made, made me want to hold his face in my hands and stare into his eyes.

"Wait," I said when he stopped the tape. "Hold on."

"I'm not going to watch this," he said, and got up to clean the mess he'd made making me dinner. His knees popped when he stood up. All that working out in the gym had made his joints old.

I grabbed ahold of his hand. "Look, Bobby. Look at you," I said. I wouldn't let go when he tried to jerk away.

"I can't," he said. "I don't wanna watch that. What'sa matter with you?"

And by that time Bobby had already come. I saw it though. Bobby's part of the video was over and now some other people were already fucking.

"Bobby," I said. I was on my knees and he was standing in front of me.

"Now what, you nut?"

"Name something about me you like, other than my body, my tits." They aren't real, so I didn't care whenever he went on and on about them.

"What are you *talking* about?"

"Just name something."

"Christ, La Donna. You're starting to get on my nerves, right? You know that, right? Lemme clean the fucking kitchen."

"Pleeease."

Bobby sighed and I let go of his hand. He crossed his big arms and then rubbed his chin that had silvery stubs mixed in with the black.

One of my favorite things to do was rub my face against all that silver and black, even though Bobby was thinking of dyeing his hair to look younger. Thirty-four and he was worried about looking old. He squinted up at the ceiling while he rubbed his chin and then a slow grin started taking over his face.

"What?" I said. I grinned back at him.

"All right. Two things. First, you know how you can't sing, right? Like, you're really shitty. Your voice is *bad.*"

I stopped grinning. "How the fuck is this a good thing, Bobby?"

"What I tell you about cussin, huh? Wait a minute. Let me finish. Your voice is bad, but you still don't stop singin."

I still wasn't grinning. "And this is good."

"Yeah."

"All right then." I was getting kind of mad. Now though, I see it was kind of a sweet thing to say, especially for Bobby. "What's the second thing?"

"OK. You know how Frankie's the fattest bastard you ever seen in your whole life?" Frankie Cappelone was Bobby's running buddy, an actor hailing from Brooklyn, too. Frankie cooked and Bobby dated some girl who worked at the same joint, is how they met. Frankie weighed about three hundred and sixty pounds and was around my height, five-seven.

"Yeah, but what's Frankie got to do with something you like about *me?*"

"I'm getting to it." Bobby was serious all off a sudden. "Listen." He shifted his weight and cracked his knuckles. "I see how you do Frank. You make him feel like he's the handsomest guy around. That's a, what?" He scratched his elbows and searched the ceiling again. "A generous thing to do. That's a real woman knows how to make a big guy like Frank feel good about himself." He was quiet for a second. "For real."

It really was one of the nicest things Bobby'd ever said to me, even if it wasn't exactly what I had in mind. And that's why I loved Bobby so. He said stuff like this, about me and Frankie. He treated me nice, cooking for me and making me take vitamins when I got sniffly, never laid a hand on me like some of the dogs I got tangled up with, even though he had the worst temper. When he looked at me, those eyes moving slow and oily over my body, I knew Bobby couldn't want anybody more than he wanted me.

The videotape was still playing. More people having more sex. I reached over and turned off the TV.

"All right, baby?" he said. "Can I clean my kitchen now?"

I was still kneeling in front of Bobby, and he traced the outline of my jaw with his fingertips. Felt like feathers when he did that, and he knew I especially liked it. He did not move for the kitchen.

On my knees in front of Bobby, I could see right before my eyes that he didn't really want to clean his kitchen, not right then. So I pulled his shorts down and handled it like the blonde didn't know how to. Like I owned it.

I never was ashamed to take my clothes off for money. Everybody who knew me knew what I did for a living. Even my mama, my brothers, my daddy. Not that they were happy about it. But the work, what I gave, was clear to me. Other people's confusion, I didn't worry about. When I met Bobby, I'd been doing it for five years because I made a lot of money, since I was twenty and graduated Glendale College. Different places in those five years, but I'd been at the Eight Ball for about six months when Bobby came in with his road dogs.

Frankie was there, and Ricky, a light-skinned, nerdy-looking brother with a mouth full of braces, always smiling. All that glitter on his teeth was practically the first thing I saw out of all three of them when they came through the door.

I was dancing to Aretha singing "Nobody Knows the Way I Feel This Morning," even though Ronnie, the manager, didn't want me to. "Don't nobody want to hear the blues when they looking at titties," he said, but then he saw the way I danced to it, shaking them like I meant it just a little bit more, and he let me alone.

I was almost done when they all walked in, on my second dance, so I was topless. The Eight Ball is small, with a tiny stage against the wall, high off the floor with a flimsy gold bar around it, so when they walked in they weren't but five or six feet away from me. People kind of turned around to look at them. I did, too, because the Eight Ball was all black and it was funny for a white guy that looked like he walked off the stories and a big, big white dude like Frankie to be walking in with their puny black bodyguard. Later Bobby, who was a regular at all kinds of strip joints, told me that because he was new to L.A. at the time and tired of westside strippers, he wanted to see some women who had some meat on their asses and thighs, and that's why he came to Crenshaw. I have plenty of meat, so he asked for a lap dance when my song ended.

After you dance? You walk around the club, say hello to all the clients, and hope they tip you. When I got off the stage and made my rounds, I saved Bobby and his crew for last. I had a lot of money tucked in my G-string by the time I got to Bobby. He smiled at me, and he had the whitest teeth you ever seen, something about the lights in the club made them glow and now I know it's because he went to the dentist and got these special treatments so he'd have the best smile for his work.

"Gentlemen," I said. "How you doing?" Bobby stopped smiling and let his eyes slide all over my body. Frankie said, "Hey. How you doing?" to my tits, and Ricky's teeth glittered at me when he took my hand and put a dollar in it. My lips got tight then, trying not to laugh, because even the women who came in tipped in my G-string.

Bobby leaned into my ear. "Do you think, can I get a lap dance with you? You dance nice." He stared at me with those honey eyes. He smelled like Dial soap. I told him to wait while I went to clean up and put my tips away. On the way to the dressing room, I bumped into Ronnie, and he asked who the white boy was. I said, "I don't know. But I'm fixin to find out."

When I came back, Frankie and Ricky were sitting close to the stage. I saw Frankie get up and tip Teresa, the new girl. Everybody called her "Little Bit" because she was so small, tiny hands and feet like a little girl.

Somebody had put Bobby off in the left corner of the club, the lap dance area. There was a big gold column that blocked the view of the corner, kind of. I walked up to Bobby and started acting. "Hey," I said, all husky and deep. I straddled him. "What can I do for you tonight?"

Bobby started acting, too. "Whatever you wanna do, you do." His teeth glowed at me, so I started working.

Couldn't find my rhythm at first, because Little Bit was dancing to some fast stuff. We're not supposed to handle the customers too much, touch them below the chest with our hands. They're not supposed to touch us either. But if you want, you can break the rules all kinds of ways. For one, you're not even supposed to straddle— straddle and sit down. But Bobby was fine and I had a feeling about him, so I did. I found where we fit and started working. I didn't listen to Little Bit's music. I made up my own in my head, held on to the back of Bobby's chair real tight, and made sure I brushed my chest against his face every now and then. Before long I started to see those faces that Bobby made, the ones I ended up knowing real well. I stared at him hard, like I was waiting for an egg to hatch but didn't stop grinding against him until he grabbed my hips and told me to stop.

"Don't move," he said.

"OK," I said, and waited for Bobby to come back to himself. I kept staring at his face, his eyes were closed. When he opened them, he didn't really look at me, he looked to the side of me, at every place but at me, like he was a boy in trouble. I said, "How'd you get that scar above your eye here?" I touched the place, a teeny slash just under his right eyebrow. Bobby touched it, too.

"Oh. Kid brother, Louie. He threw a rock at me after I beat his ass for talking back to Ma."

"You're lucky he didn't hit you in the eye."

"No, that fucker's lucky." Bobby shook his head and smiled at me when he finally looked me in the eyes. He tried to sound like a hard-ass when he was talking about his brother, but you know how people say stuff about folks in a way that lets you know they're crazy about the person? They can't help it? Bobby was crazy about his little brother.

"Louie," I said, like I had decided something. I don't know why. Then I said, "Hey. Look." I felt around my right eye. "I got one, too. Fell on the corner of a glass table when I was six. Mama said, all right, keep playing around that table and see what happens. She kissed me when I started crying, though."

Bobby took my face in his hands and pulled my chin down so he could get a better look at my eye.

"You ever notice," I said, "that a lot of people have some sort of scar around their eyes, like you and me?"

"What? You notice this lap dancin?"

"No. Just in life. Walking around. Seeing things."

Bobby scooted forward in his chair and moved me around with him. He grabbed a handful of my braids and pulled on them, not hard, though.

"You're getting heavy on my lap here."

"Sorry." I stood up and Bobby stood up with me. He untucked his T-shirt from his jeans.

"I like you," he said, to my eyes, not my tits. He gave me sixty dollars and went to the bathroom.

Before he left, he asked me, "What's your name?" When I told him, he said it back to me. "La Donna." He said it again. "La Donna."

Two weeks later, after him coming back again and again, Bobby asked me out and after that we were together. For a whole year. Even though I wasn't the first black girl Bobby'd dated, I was the first one he finally told his mama and daddy about, "So they could get their heart attacks out early," Bobby said. When I asked if he'd told them about the stripping, he asked me if I was a wise guy.

He got it in his mind that since I was his girl, I shouldn't be stripping. "I don't want you touching other guys, showing other guys your tits, guys touching you, you making guys come. If you're with me, you ain't working at the Eight Ball," he said. "You're going to have to quit it," he said. So I did. I thought he was the one, and if he was the one, I had to keep him. And I guess he sort of had a point about my tits being in some other man's face, but that really had nothing to do with me and him home alone. Just like all the films and magazines he'd done, that I'd seen, didn't hardly remind me of Bobby when I looked at them. Still, he had carried on, hollering all this through the bathroom door, pounding on it for me to come out.

"Fuck you, Bobby! Fuck you!" I screamed. I was so mad. He was the one doing porno, not me. He didn't have the guts to tell people what his job was, and I never sweat him about it, because he did his job and he still came home a good person. Just like me. "Fuck you!" I screamed one more time.

"Hey!" He kicked a dent in the door. He could have kicked it down if he wanted. "What I tell you about that mouth!"

On Saturdays, after Bobby went to confession at this big Catholic church off of Franklin, he liked to cook big dinners. It'd be Frankie, Bobby, Ricky and me, sitting around on Bobby's floor, sometimes we'd eat at my apartment, too. I liked those Saturdays before I had to go back to my office job and start the week. Sundays didn't count because they were wasted on dreading Monday. The office was a weird place to be because I'd been dancing for so long. I missed the club; all the girls, how we used to look out for each other, understand each other. Sometimes, somebody had to be a bitch, but I even missed that. None of my friends liked Bobby, so Bobby, Ricky, and Frankie were the next best thing to girlfriends. And the guys didn't like the one person I met and liked at work, Angela. She was the only one who knew what I used to do, and since Bobby was picking up the slack from what I used to make dancing, she said, what was I complaining about? I got to thinking she had a point. Dancing was just a job. Bobby was my partner in life. He was only looking out for me. How could I be mad at that? My back was starting to hurt from working, anyway.

Angela was nice to me, and I liked her, but once, I had her over to my place to eat with the guys. Bobby, I caught checking out her long black hair and her ass once or twice. And Frankie thought she was snotty. After she left he said, "What? She supposed to be fuckin royalty or something? Her ass powdered with fuckin gold dust? Class with a 'K,' that one." I never asked Angela over for Saturday dinner again, but once in a while we hung out, because I got lonely and because Bobby and Frankie I wasn't going to let tell me who to be friends with.

One Saturday night Bobby was excited because two of his spreads had come out at the same time. We had them out, laughing at some of the poses Bobby was in. My favorite spread was in a magazine called *Slick* and it was this little story of Bobby getting stopped by a traffic cop wearing a miniskirt and stilettoes. The title said, "Busted! A Sexed-Up Slut in Uniform, This Cop Is Ready for Action." I liked this one because Bobby was supposed to be beat down by this girl who couldn't be more than five-two. On the second page of the spread, Bobby was standing next to a Porsche they got from somewhere. The cop had her hands in his pants. "She orders a strip search and demands total submission." I read the sentences underneath the pictures out loud, and Bobby said, "You think you're funny, right?"

On the next page? Somehow they'd gotten from the Porsche on the street to a brick basement somewhere. "Back to the wall, cuffed and compliant, he obeys her kinky commands." Bobby was wearing the cop's hat in this shot. He was chained to the wall, too, some kind of way.

"Donna," Frankie said, "slide that this way." He was sitting in the one chair Bobby had in the whole apartment. He looked like he'd grown into that chair. Been sitting in it his whole life. He cleared his throat and put some of the actor into it. Frankie had a nice deep voice when he wanted to. Made the room vibrate, it seemed like. "This is one X-rated interrogation that could lead to repeat offenses." He sang it, almost. Then he sat back in his chair like somebody had let the air out of him.

"Fuckin Royal Shakespeare Academy, you fat bastard," Bobby said. He threw a towel at Frankie. Frank got lines in real movies because he was a character actor. He had an old-fashioned face, the kind of face you see in black and white movies. Frankie had black hair that he kept real short. His eyes jumped out at you and looked at you like they were connecting dots all over you. Sometimes, in a certain light, anybody could see that his eyes were nicer than Bobby's, sadder, more clear. When he laughed, he had a big gap between his front teeth, made him seem more happy than he really was. Frank always acted more happy than he really was. In a way, that made him more interesting than Bobby. I never said that to anybody because Bobby was jealous of Frankie. He loved Frankie like blood, he always said, like a brother. But he didn't like it that Frank didn't have to take off his clothes to have a line or two in a Hollywood movie. I thought that was where all that fat stuff came from. Every time you turned around, Bobby was calling Frankie fat, like you could miss that about Frank if you looked at him.

I knew, too, that Bobby would tell Frankie about all the different kinds of sex we'd had, to rub it in a little bit. One thing Bobby was doing that Frankie couldn't. I knew they talked about it, because after the first night I spent at Bobby's apartment, Frankie teased me about hearing that I liked the breakfast of champions. I told Bobby that he had a big mouth, that it was nobody's business what time of the day I gave him blow jobs, and Bobby told me that Frankie was his boy and that I had to get used to them talking.

The night we were kidding Bobby, Ricky was sitting on the floor with his ankles crossed over each other and his face resting on his knuckles. "Let's see the magazine," he said. He was a tight-ass, but I liked him because he was so serious and respectful. He always acted like, if I was stripping, I might as well be teaching or performing brain surgery. He was still a hammy actor when he wanted to be, but he usually saved it for commercials. He checked out Bobby's spread. "Hm," he said. "This come-shot looks funny." He scratched his nose.

"What do you mean?" Bobby snatched the magazine from Ricky, worried. He thought Ricky was saying that his face looked funny.

"It doesn't look authentic." Ricky blinked once. For an actor, he hardly ever had any kind of look to his face than a smile every once in a while.

"What don't?" Bobby's voice was getting high.

"The semen," Ricky said, patient, like he was explaining math.

Bobby let out a big breath, and Frank snorted. "Sea-man. Fuckin Bill Cosby over here."

"It ain't real, Ricky," Bobby said, disgusted. You would have thought Ricky was the biggest fool on the planet.

I'd been laying flat on my back, rubbing my belly and trying to get Bobby's stuffed pasta shells to digest quicker. But I sat up when I heard what Bobby said.

"Let me see that again." In the last frame, Bobby was standing over a black-haired woman with beautiful skin, was the first thing I noticed. Or, she could have been airbrushed. Looked like she was decorated with watery icing. "This isn't *real?*"

"Listen everybody." Bobby said it like he was making a big announcement. "How many times I gotta tell you? *It ain't real.* Glue, they use sometimes. If you're havin a bit of trouble. Or even if you're not," he added real quick. "It's just for looks."

Frankie folded his hands over his stomach. "I knew that."

I didn't.

The work Bobby did never upset me that much. Well, maybe a little bit sometimes. I never thought about it too hard. When I did think about it, the way Bobby was with me, the way he always treated me right, came out on top. But this girl with glue dripped all over her body? Wasn't that strange? I thought it was strange, not to be able to tell the difference, to be fooled like that when I didn't expect it. I should know the fake stuff when I see it. I got quiet thinking about the picture. How can I explain it? Like, the glue and Bobby kneeling over the woman with his dick in his hand, posed and everything, to me, it was all cheaper and more nasty than people think of the *real* come and *real* fucking on a video. You feel sorry or something, for the people in the picture, and the people looking at the picture.

"Bobby," I said, "why didn't they just have you work on yourself or something until you could finish the job?" Bobby shrugged. He was yawning, getting ready to kick Frankie and Ricky out.

Frankie said, "Doll, people ain't got hours and fucking days to wait on a drop a two from this guy." Bobby raised his middle finger. "Plus," Frankie said, "I happen to know, that sometimes the real stuff ain't as pretty, ain't as dramatic looking. You gotta embellish."

All night, those pasta shells didn't seem to want to digest. "You poisoned me," I moaned to Bobby after Ricky and Frankie left. I was curled up in a ball. My stomach was hurting from the cheese and pasta. Bobby loved to take care of me when I was sick so I laid it on. The more I carried on, the more helpless I was, the more attention

I got from Bobby. He loved being in charge of me that way, any way. He'd already made me take Pepto Bismol and kept kissing me on my forehead.

"Ohhhh," I moaned.

"La Donna, baby, you ain't dying here."

"Bohhhhbby," I whined good. He lay down and curled into me. He held my hand and whispered in my ear. His breath felt good, warmed me all over like I was drinking tea.

"La Donna Sherida Jackson," he whispered. "I, Roberto Charles Cantadopolous, won't let nothing happen to you, baby." He kissed my neck. I liked when he said all three of my names. Sounded to me like he was invested in me. He rubbed my stomach and talked to me low until I wasn't so curled up anymore. He kept on until I started hmmmmm-ing. Hmmmmmmmm was in my throat until I was purring like a kitty cat.

Frankie claimed he hadn't had a girlfriend in four years because he'd been fat for four years. He said when his mother died in a car wreck when he was twenty-seven, he just stopped caring about what he ate or didn't eat, let himself go. "I became the fattest fuck you ever saw," he said. "I swear to God." Plus, he was good at cooking, so. There you go. He got out of Brooklyn after drinking himself into trouble and started acting after somebody in the café he cooked in said he had a face. Frankie's got a face for real. Not TV story pretty like Bobby's, but still a face. A face you like.

He and Bobby stayed thick. Right up under each other all the time. Frankie made jokes about the reputation of Greeks, but when I said they were spending so much time together, were they fucking, they didn't think I was funny.

"Careful, there, hot ass," Frankie said.

"What I tell you, hanh?" Bobby said. Always the two of them against me.

I got to be crazy about Frankie, too. He got to be *my* road dog. The best and the worst time I ever had with Frank, we all were supposed to get together downtown, but Bobby stood us up. Both Bobby and Frankie had been on the set of the film Bobby was working on in some loft, because Frankie wanted to watch the sex, even if it *was* Bobby. I waited for those two at the bar of the Biltmore Hotel, sad over the worst day; faxing, and faxing and filing for a snobby architect. I was already into my second extra spicy Bloody Mary when Frankie found me.

"Where's Bobby?" I said. I was disappointed.

"I'm fine, thanks, Doll." Frankie sat down next to me on the purple velvet couch. He ran his hand over the arm.

"How you doin, Frank?" I leaned over and kissed him on the cheek.

"There you go. That's more like it."

I still wanted to know where Bobby was. I hadn't seen him in two days because of this new job he had. Frankie picked up my drink and wiped the lipstick off the rim. "I'm dry," he said before he took a sip. He made a face and fanned his mouth.

"Jesus. I'm never letting you in my kitchen. You coloreds with the hot sauce."

"Fuck you, Frank." I punched him on the arm.

"I'm gonna tell on you to Bobby, with the 'fuck you.'" He gave me back my drink. "The strudel's workin late, by the way." He called Bobby strudel sometimes. "He's lookin like forty miles of French road, that guy. Plenty of glue on that set." He winked at me.

I sank down in the couch and looked at the pictures on the walls. Old Hollywood pictures. Jimmy Stewart, Bette Davis, Audrey

Hepburn. Lots of group shots at the Oscars in the '30s and '40s. I thought of Bobby with his dick between some woman's tits. I raised a finger to order another drink, but Frankie slapped it down. He pulled a silver flask from the pocket of his jean jacket, and the jacket was so big that you couldn't tell he also had a bottle in his other pocket.

"Have a pop a this," he said.

I took the flask. "What is this?"

"Jack Daniel's."

"Jack mixed with Mary, Frank? Nah. I don't think so." I tried to give it back to him.

"C'mahn. Have a pop." He pushed it back to me.

"Nah. I don't feel like it."

"C'mahhn. Just one pop. It'll loosen you up some, take your mind off that douche."

I shook the flask to see if I could hear the liquid in there. I took a drink but tried to hide that I was drinking in case anybody saw me. The bar was a nice one, and I didn't want anybody to think I didn't have any home training. After I had my sip, Frankie leaned back, satisfied, and I ordered another Bloody Mary.

That was the night Frank and I drank ourselves silly. The first half of the night he made me laugh with Brooklyn stories, but by closing time we weren't laughing so much. We were listening to the sound of the glasses being washed and put away in the kitchen behind the bar. Sounded, almost, like the glasses were being broken behind the swinging doors. And they'd turned off the jazz, so the quiet and the glasses being put away made *us* quiet.

Then, too, I was thinking of this secret that Frankie let slip out, due to all the pops of Jack he'd had. On his birthday that'd passed two months ago? Bobby paid for Frankie to go to this masseuse woman that gave him a hand job, somewhere off of Beverly Boulevard. Frankie hadn't been with a woman for free in years, so really, so what about the massage and everything? That was the best gift Bobby could think of to give him. But why didn't Bobby tell me about it, I wondered. He told Frankie *everything* we did. He didn't care about putting my business in the streets. Thinking about it and thinking, I hardly noticed they were kicking us out the bar, time to go. When Frankie stood up and pulled me off the couch, I swear he looked like one of the pictures on the wall. Kind of blurry, but kind of classic. Like he belonged. Or maybe not. It was two o'clock in the morning and hard to tell.

Frankie drove me home in his crushed-up car. A *small* car, way too small for Frankie. A red two-door Dodge Colt from 1982 or something. Didn't look like Frank could get his foot in the car, forget about his whole body. But for one hundred dollars, Frankie did good. On the way home we sang "The Little Drummer Boy," even though Christmas was five months away.

"Goddamn your voice is bad," he said. "By the grace of God, at least you got a nice tail on you." I pinched his arm, but he didn't act like he felt it.

He pulled up in front of the courtyard of my building and turned off the car. "Doll, don't make me get outta this thing and walk you to the door, right? We ain't got all night."

I laughed at Frank and kissed him on the cheek.

"What? I make you laugh?"

"Yeah."

"You like that, hanh?"

"Yeah."

Frank put both hands on the steering wheel. "Well, do something for me then, Doll."

I had my keys in one hand and my other hand on the door handle. I was ready to get out but I waited. I didn't like Frank's tone. I'd heard it before.

"Frank."

"Shut up for a minute. Right here." He touched his lips with his thick fingers. "Give me a kiss."

"No."

"It ain't gonna kill you."

"Goodnight, Frankie," I said. I banged the raggedy door shut and stumbled up the walkway and through my front door. He waited until I was all the way in before he drove off.

There wasn't even a message from Bobby on my machine. I wondered where he was, what he was doing, worrying about him, worrying about him working without the cameras rolling. I called him, but there was no answer.

I washed my face, brushed my teeth, stared out my living room window at the dirty pool in the courtyard. When the phone rang, I said "Bobby?"

"No, Doll."

"I'm worried about Bobby, Frankie."

"Don't. There was a message from that douche when I got home. He said he was tired, drunk from all the cheap champagne crap on the set. Said he was going to pass out."

"Well . . . Why didn't he call me?"

"Fuck if I know," Frankie said. His voice was low and soft, made me want to crawl into bed. Then he said, "What're you, gettin ready for bed?"

"I been ready."

"Yeah? What're you wearin?"

"Frank."

"C'mahn. What you got going on over there?"

"*Nothing*. I got nothing on. I'm going to *bed*."

I tried to go to bed, but I couldn't, because Frankie wouldn't let me off the phone. He got next to me, whispering stories about how he was lonely, wanted a girl of his own, stories about what he pictured us doing, sometimes while I might be sitting right there in front of him, blowing my nose or whatever.

"Just this one time, Doll," he said. "Talk to me."

I got into bed and pulled the covers tight around my neck like when I was a kid and afraid of vampires biting my neck to suck my blood.

"Tell me some stuff. Talk to me sexy."

I pulled the covers all the way over my head and hunched over. It was completely black and I couldn't see anything. I said, "Frankie, your face is like art. I love it when you make me laugh." I made my voice soft like his.

"You're not doing it for me, here. Stop playing around, La Donna." But I wasn't playing around. I started to play around after Frank hollered at me, though. The whole thing took five minutes. Frankie, I said, you make me hot, I want you, Frank. Yeah, Daddy, harder. And on and on until Frank said he was going to come. "Talk to me, let me hear you," he said. I screamed and moaned into the phone like I thought he wanted me to.

All I could hear was Frankie's breathing for a minute, then he blew a big breath into the phone. "Thanks for helping me out there, Doll." He was quiet for a second. "Did you really come?"

"Me?" I almost laughed until I figured out he wasn't messing with me. "Yeah, I did," I said, thinking Bobby would be proud of me if he ever knew. I didn't want him to, though. This was between me and Frankie, a thing I gave him when he needed it. I felt bad for Frank. I asked him please, to promise not to tell Bobby.

"Don't worry, Donna. On my mother's grave. I swear," Frankie said. So I went to sleep on top of my covers, feeling generous, like Bobby said.

Sometimes you need to be just a little bit older to figure things out. Even two or three days older might do it. I really thought Frankie would want to do the phone thing only once, but he started calling me all the time. All the time like maybe eight times we did it. Something else I learned since I'm older: if a man starts picking on you about the things he used to love about you, the end is beginning. Like, La Donna, your ass is getting big, when bigger used to be better. Say then, you lose the weight fast for him and he complains about stretch marks you got because of that. In your head, you say, kiss my black ass, because you either get thin, with stretch marks, or thick, with a big ass. You don't get both. But if you're afraid he's going to leave you, even if you're starting to want to leave yourself, then you don't say a word.

I had to practically force Bobby to spend time with me anymore. I worried, I thought that he'd met some girl on the job, but I couldn't get anything out of Ricky or Frankie. My last birthday with Bobby, about a month after I got started on the phone with Frank, he only offered to take me out to dinner because I dropped hints like you wouldn't believe. We drove to a restaurant called Olio e Aceto in his convertible that someone had slashed the top of the night before. So Bobby was mad. Bobby mad made me want to lie down with him sometimes. Sometimes, Bobby mad was ugly. That night, I didn't know which one it was, I couldn't tell. I watched him grind his teeth.

The place I wanted to go to ended up having nasty food, but it was pretty on the outside. They had guys out parking your car and everything. I thought it would turn out to be something good, that place. I guess I was wrong. Bobby took home a doggy bag, even though he said it was "the world's shittiest food he'd ever had in his whole entire fuckin life on the planet earth." I don't know how that was my fault, but it was. And my dress showed "too much titty," and my lipstick looked "trampy," and the blouse he gave me for my birthday, the style, the statement, the material, even the size, none of it had anything to do with me. He picked it out in two minutes, you could tell.

When we were leaving the restaurant, Bobby stopped just before we got outside and asked me to hold his bag. I took it and waited for him to lace his shoes or whatever it was he'd given me the bag to do, but he just kept walking.

"Hey," I said, "wait a minute. Why'd you give me this?" Before he answered me, Bobby noticed his reflection in a window and smoothed down his hair.

"I just don't feel like carrying it," he said, and walked out of the restaurant.

More than any gift, I wanted a massage from Bobby on my birthday. His hands, his fingertips were like drugs. Bobby walked straight to his chair after we got home from dinner and sat down without a word. He twirled his keys around his finger and still worked his jaw. His mood made me nervous. My stomach started acting funny on me, but I still put on a Prince record, "If I Was Your Girlfriend," and stood in front of him. I started stripping to the music. He liked it if I danced only for him. He kept his face tight, but he was rubbing his palms on his jeans, so I knew. I straddled him and worked him until he was hard, but I wanted this to last. I asked him for a massage. Bobby looked into my eyes for a long time, waiting to tell me something, waiting for me to tell him something.

"Ask Frankie," he said.

I crossed my arms over my chest. "Ask Frank what?"

"For a massage."

"What are you talking about?" Bobby pushed at my hips, so I got off his lap and sat down on the floor because I couldn't stand any more.

"I'm talking about calling up Frank and having him work you over."

A second, maybe two, I sat in front of Bobby, not knowing what was happening. Then I understood, that when people swear on their mother's grave, they may as well swear on a stack of Bibles or cross their heart. What people think of the weight of their own words is what keeps a promise. Not dead people. And then I had to understand, work it all out sitting there in front of Bobby, how he could think less of me when all I tried to be was good.

This is how: Bobby told me how he knew about the Frankie phone thing, but I broke it down in my head like two men measuring their actors' dicks, when it all came down to it. Frankie drunk one night, bragging about the last role he'd landed. "You ain't that good, you fat bastard. So what, you got a part?" is what Bobby said. Then, Frankie bragging he was so good that he could make people feel things they didn't even know they felt, especially women. Break any woman down just like that. Get her to feel so sorry for him she'd take care of him over the phone, for example, is what Frankie said. Even La Donna, he said, he could break.

I sat there with my legs in a circle in front of me and crossed at my ankles, how I always liked to sit. Bobby's honey eyes kept moving from my face to the space between my legs, back and forth, still working that jaw like he felt like throwing me out or fucking me. And that's another time when I was just a few minutes older than before to know that me and Bobby were no good any more.

I started crying, hard, like kids when they can't get enough air down their throats to keep on crying. They suck in little breaths like hiccups, and once they start they can't stop, until they pass out, wasted. And there I was sitting and crying even though I was so mad I could have smashed those perfect teeth of his, maybe because I was so mad and couldn't smash them in was why I couldn't stop crying.

"Bobby, I was faking it!" I mean I really screamed at him. I was just about through with him. *Had* it with him. "Me and Frankie weren't even in the same zip codes when he came. He never even touched me."

"No, but he got to you. He might as well of touched you. Same difference." Bobby was still working his jaw, but he was speaking real low, like he wasn't sure of what he was saying. His knees popped when he stood up and that made me want to go to him for a minute, and then that same difference thing he said popped into my head. Then I wasn't just a dancer that was a good person. I was a ho. Bobby fucked women for money, wasn't no actor or no good person, and Frankie—Frankie was a fat bastard like Bobby said. Thinking like that made me even sadder, because that wasn't the truth, not exactly, but Bobby made me wonder in the first place, breaking everything down the way he did.

I cussed Bobby like you wouldn't believe. I didn't care what I called him. I screamed until my throat hurt. He had to grab my hands to calm me down. He lay me down and touched me, his way of saying he was sorry, but it was too late. He started with my feet and worked all the way up to my eyes, little circles around the corners of my eyes. He kissed me all over and over and over again on the tip of my nose. "I'm sorry, La Donna. I'm so sorry. I'm sorry, I'm sorry," he said. Soft. He held my hand in his and kissed it, but it was too late for me to feel anything anymore.

I'm still dancing, dating a brother, an art history student who thinks it's cool I dance—he says. He came in with his boys, thinking how entertaining it all would be to see some strippers. It was a "novelty," he said. I still don't know about that. Anyway, give me a room full of men I never seen before in my life, shaking my titties just as hard as I can, before you give me that room with me and Bobby alone with him working his jaw.

I think about it, and see us there on the floor of Bobby's apartment, a good-looking man with a perfect actor face, holding a woman like she was his heart, his life. If you'd seen us, what would you have thought? Would we have looked like a scene from a movie? Two people in love? To you, what would we seem to be?

mouthful of sorrow

Why don't you come and sit with me for a
spell, keep me company? That's right. Right c'here on the porch
with me. It's evenings like this I get to thinking bout things. When
the heat start to break and the sky get that gray-blue in it, touching
the tops of the trees out yonder. Best time of day in the summertime.
I like to just sit back, listen to them bad children playing, cussing,
and carrying on over in the holler. There they go, too. Hear how they
voices carry? That echo almost picking at you, the sound of it making you sad and happy at the same time.

Now ain't that something you remember me! You wasn't nothing but a little bitty thing last time you come round from California. You grown and look just like your mama. You her picture! Looking like a lady, too. Where them scabby knees and pigtails at? You ain't got no babies, is you? Good. That's all right. Ain't no need of you rushing it, hear? You ain't but what? Seventeen? Take all the time you need, honey. Sit right c'here with me and pass some time.

Bout this time I start looking for the little spirits. That's what the lightning bugs look like early nighttime. What you say? Fireflies? They was always lightning bugs to us when we was coming up. At the start of night they come out drifting and floating and blinking such a little bit at first you ain't even sure you seen em, like something you caught out the corner of your eye. Put me in mind of little ghosts. Little ghosts just trying to find they way.

But listen at me just running my mouth. Honey, you ain't got to sit up on this porch with this old lady if you don't want to. I ain't even that old, but you wouldn't know that, with this raggedy housecoat I'm wearing, house shoes, hair all over my head. I'm telling you the truth, seem like I woke up old one day.

You know where them kids is playing, down in the holler? Used to be a little joint down there called Lonnie's. Everybody'd be down to Lonnie's on a Saturday night. Get all dressed up, even though the place wasn't nothing but a shack, really. If you was looking for somebody Saturday night, you knew where they'd be at.

Now hand me my spit can. Look at you, handing it to me with your little finger all turned up like you giving me my slop jar. I used to do the same thing with Mama, my nose all wrinkled up, talking bout *I ain't never gone dip snuff.* And here I am. Don't talk bout what you ain't never going to do. You make a liar out yourself every time.

One of the meanest tricks of life is not knowing what's gone be the last time you do something or see somebody. You be talking bout "See you tomorrow" and the next thing you know, they be dead or gone. That ain't right. Might be the Lord's doing, but I don't got to like everything he do.

What's on my mind when I'm telling you this is my best friend, Addie. You talk bout being close. Honey, let me tell you, we was tight. You hardly saw one of us without the other right up under her. People always used to pick at us and ask which one of us was the man, trying to be funny, you know, because we was always together. But back then, I didn't b'lieve I loved her like that. Shoot, I had me a man, had Mosely. I loved her like she was my sister, cept maybe a little bit more. Wasn't nothing we wouldn't do for each other. Seem like whatever one of us needed, the other had it to give, before you knew what it was you wanted your own self! I knew her like you know how to walk. Course we sho could scrap from time to time, too. Used to fight each other like we was crazy, but bother one of us and you had both of us to try to whup.

Let me tell you what I'm talking bout. When Mama first started letting me go out, one of the Bradley boys, Bobby Jean, thought he was gone get something from me, and you know what I'm talking bout. I fought him on it. So he popped me, and I mean good. Had my eye all black and swole up. Mama said I must of acted like I had the same thing on my mind that he did, else he wouldn't of tried nothing. But Addie! We caught up with Bobby Jean one night down at Lonnie's. She called his name out real nice and soft, and when he turned around she kicked him in his information. That boy fell to his knees, squeezing out tears, while I kicked him in his behind. And never did a thing to us. Not a thing. Come to me a week later, talking bout he was sorry!

But when me and Addie fought each other!

You prolly too young to remember Mr. Burl Spicer, lived up the road a piece in that shack on the edge of the creek. He dead now. When my daddy passed, he and Mama started helping each other out. He used to bring Mama well water, and for that she'd cook him up fried chicken every Sunday and have me run it to him. He was just as nice as he could be. One Sunday he come around the road when me and Addie was playing patty-cake. We was bout nine years old at the time, singing our little rhymes and cuttin up, not paying Mr. Burl no mind, till we saw the kitty cat, all gray and fluffy, tucked in the bib pocket of his overalls.

"Oohh look, a kitty!" Addie said, and started petting it and kissing it on the nose and carrying on like she ain't never seen no cat before.

"I brung it for Sticks," he said, grinning at me. That's what he used to call me to pick at me. "I told you, soon as they was old enough, I'd brang you one."

"Thank you, sir," I said, and took the cat. I never really did like cats. I didn't think Mr. Burl was going to give me one. Shoot, when I saw them kitty cats and was talking to Mr. Burl about them things, I was just talking, really. To me, cats is uppity, act like they don't want to be round you, don't want you giving them love and attention. I ain't got no use for all that.

Well, Mama must of heard us talking to Mr. Burl cause she come out on the porch with his chicken and set it down on the railing. "Spicer," she say she said to him, "long as you knowed me you know I hate cats, so what you mean giving that chile a cat!" She put her hands on her hips, cutting out any kind of talk about it.

The sun itself just about broke out on Addie's face. "Give it to me." She grabbed it from me. "My mama likes cats and she ain't gone mind."

Well, I jerked it back from her. She was just acting all silly over that damn cat, excuse my mouth. "He didn't give it to you," I hollered. "He give it to me!"

Addie looked at me like I'd lost my mind and grabbed that poor kitty cat back and, honey, we just went at it, pulling and pushing and the cat scratching us both up, then Mr. Burl trying to get in on it to break us up. It was a mess, I'm telling you the truth. I had Addie good by the hair when she broke from me.

"You make me sick!" she said, and threw that poor little kitty cat across the road. It knocked over Mr. Burl's chicken plate that was setting on the porch railing before it hit the wall of my house and slid down the wall, dead. The chicken plate was making that wobbly sound, you know how plates and things do, wobbling faster and faster till they stop and then you don't hear nothing.

"Cain't nobody have it now," Addie said. "How you like that?"

Well, that shocked everybody, even Mama, who'd seen and done some things in her life, let me tell you. I just kept staring at the cat on the porch. It looked all fake like one of them animals you win at the fair.

Mama said to Addie, "I think you best go home, Miss Raleigh."

"Yessum," Addie said, and started down the road, like all Mama had said was have a good time at the picture show.

Mr. Burl and Mama give each other the eyebrows, and then Mr. Burl dusted off his chicken, said God made dirt and dirt don't hurt, thanked Mama, and went on about his business. Mama stared down the road after Addie, wiped her face with the rag she'd tucked in her chest, and then told me to bury the cat out behind the house here. Next day, me and Addie got together like usual, jumping rope and whatnot, and we never said another word about the kitty cat.

That's the kind of fights we had, fights that never made no kind of sense. And most of the time, Addie come out on top, but one time she made me so mad, I had to tell her like it T-I-*is*. That girl was wrong like two left shoes and she knowed it.

To this day I cain't see no baldheaded man and not think of Lucien Smith. *Honey.* You talking bout *fine.* He wasn't nothing but a boy, round seventeen like me and Addie, but I'm telling you the *truth* he was bout the blackest man you ever did see, and back then, wasn't no saying it loud you was black and proud. Most of the girls in our class was running after David Spears, with the yellow skin and gray eyes, hair all sandy and wavy. But to tell you the truth, David Spears wasn't all that fine. Might of been closer to white than the rest of us, but that's all he had going for him. Lucien, though, honey. His skin was just as smooooth. Kept his head clean, cause he say he didn't want to worry about no hair. And folks teased him, too, cause that wasn't the style—less you was an old man! Called him Skeeball, Shinehead. Just did him wrong. And here I was. I loved me some Lucien Smith. Addie knowed it, too.

Anyway, Lucien heard tell what I thought of him, and he finally come round to asking me to the show one day when me and Addie was walking home from school. Course I said yes before the chile could even get the words out, but I was scared to go with him alone, so I ast if Addie could come on along with us. Lucien didn't look happy about that, but he said he didn't mind.

Well. That Saturday roll around and Addie'd told me she was gone meet us at the thee-ater. We waited and waited till we couldn't wait no more, we was gone have to go up to the balcony and get our seats before it got too full. Black folks could only sit up in the balcony, and if those seats got full, you was out of luck cause they wasn't gone let no black folks sit down there with no white people. But just as we fixing to go on up and get us some seats, who coming up the street dressed like she was a ten-cent ho from the big city? And don't ast me where she got them clothes, cause I don't know. But they was tight, and they was loud, and Addie's lips was painted on looked like permanent! You talking about red!

She walked up to me and Lucien with her hips swinging like she knocking down walls on either side, all breathless, talking bout "Sorry I'm late."

"Late!" I say. "What in the world you got on!"

"What?" Addie say, like she was all surprised. Like she don't know what I'm talking bout. She turned to Lucien then, and looked at him a little too long for my taste. He was looking back, too!

How she gone make me feel like I'm wearing a potato sack from Mama's kitchen on my first date with the man I thought I'd die from wanting so bad?!

"Oooh. You heifa!" I said, and just commenced to snatching at anything I could get my hands on. Honey, folks gathered. Finally Lucien broke us up, and neither one of us ventually ended up with him. He started going with some little mousy thing later, and that ain't last but a minute.

Mama got after me when I got home later, cause word travel fast. Say she better not hear of me acting common like that again, fighting in the streets over some man. "We may be on the poor side, Maybonne, but we know how to act like we got some sense. Womens fighting over a man is just as trifling as can be. You don't let no man come between you and your friends. Not no good friends. You hear?"

Sho nuff, me and Addie was thick as thieves not two days after.

You know, you can reach the point of hating a person as much as you love em. Hate em for making you lose yourself in em cause you want to be just like em and have everything they got. I had that kind of love for Addie, and Addie had that kind of love for Fella, thought he hung the moon.

Wouldn't of been that bad for me if Addie had loved somebody worth all she was giving him. I wasn't the only one heard about Fella carrying on with some girl over in Nashville, and before that, somebody else. Seem like as long as I been knowing Fella—and he sho was fine, ain't no need of me lying bout that—he was always sticking his business in some woman when he already had one woman or another to tend to. I guess cause he was so hard to hold down, Addie's way of thinking was that he was that much finer the prize. She had him, didn't she? And she thought since she had him he wouldn't step out on her cause she wasn't like them other girls. She was special. She was, too, but that man wouldn't of knowed special if it walked up to him, handed that fool one of them business cards, and introduced itself!

Well, nobody told Addie about Fella carrying on, least of all me. That chile saw what she wanted to see and I'd a rather had somebody cut my heart out than to hurt Addie. You know what I said bout one of us always giving what the other one needed? Well, she needed not to know bout Fella.

My last night down to Lonnie's, me and Mosely hadn't been too long through the door when Addie snuck up behind me and smacked me on my behind. Lonnie's was always dark and smoky, but I could see her little pixie face grinning at me. Still can sometimes.

"Maybonne, girl, I got something to tell you." She grabbed my hand and drug me through the café to the bathroom. Right there, her grabbing my hand and leading me is just as clear. B. B. King was singing "Every Day I Have the Blues" from the jukebox, and Squeak was getting his tail whupped at dominoes by John Lee like he always did. Folks was drinking and dancing and having a good time mostly cause Lonnie kept pouring em drinks. And I stole one quick glance at Mosely and Fella up at the bar. Fella was looking me dead in my eye. He was stroking his shiny mustache and grinning, them white white teeth against his black skin. He winked at me with one of his great big eyes the color of a caramel apple, before Addie jerked me into the bathroom.

"Girl," I said, "what you mean just a pulling me all through the café? Shoot. Stretched my sweater all out of shape." I was trying to fix myself up and wasn't paying her no mind.

"I'm gone have Fella's baby, May," she said, looking all bashful and proud. "Fella say he going to take me with him to California."

Thoughts was coming in my head and leaving before I had a chance to make anything of em. Couldn't even open my mouth. Me and Addie come up together from babies and I never thought bout a time when we wouldn't be together.

Addie stared at me, her mouth real tight like she was about to get mad. She said, "What? Ain't you happy for me? You hear what I say? Fella taking me out of this piss-pot town!"

Wasn't no way in the world I could have been happy for that girl cause I was selfish and thinking about myself. I started crying like a baby. "You cain't go!"

Addie stepped up to me and wrapped her arms round me. We was a funny picture to folks coming into the bathroom, tall and skinny as I was with Addie not even coming up to my chest, trying to comfort me.

"Ain't you even happy bout my baby?" she ast with a little smile. When I didn't give her no answer she pulled a cigarette out of her purse, lit it, and put it in my mouth. She untied the scarf round her neck and used it to wipe my eyes and my cheeks. That scarf was her favorite one, too. Let me see, bright blue with red specks in it. When she was done, she tied it back round her neck, smeared makeup on it and all.

Addie looked down at my shoes and said, "I see you wearing them old run-over loafers. Ain't even got no pennies in em."

"Forget you, heifa," I said to her. "Who you posed to be in them muddy white pumps back up here in these sticks, Doris Day or somebody?" I took a long drag on the Pall Mall she give me and blowed it out right slow. We both was laughing. Then I stopped cause I remembered. I went from sad to mad then, hating Fella for taking my friend away, thinking bout how Addie was giving me up for him. He wasn't even worth the spit in my mouth.

"That man," I said. I put my cigarette out in the sink and leaned up against it. "That man ain't all you think he is, girl." I couldn't look her in the eyes. I was looking at them green walls, the paint all chipped and peeling, the lightbulb hanging from the ceiling. Moths was throwing themselves at it. There was another girl in there with us, in the stall across from the sink, but I didn't care. I knowed with them words that I had done got it started. You couldn't start no mess with Addie and not finish it.

She crossed her arms and shifted her weight on her right hip, her head all tilted, squinting at me. "Ain't all I think he is? What you talking bout?"

"Throwing your life away for that dog."

"Dog!" Addie took a couple steps toward me. I stepped back.

"Listen, I know you better than I know my own self. You starting all kinds of mess cause you jealous of Fella. I love you, but this shit I ain't going to let you do."

I said, "You know me. Then you know I ain't lying when I say Fella be with some other woman when he ain't with you."

Addie pressed both her hands on her belly like she was trying to hold it down. Her eyes got all small and tight, like she was trying to see something she couldn't. Then she said, real low, "You a evil cow. I don't b'lieve nothing you telling me."

That girl in the stall, Georgia Shields, come out finally. She said to Addie, "You the last to know, girl," and got out of there quick and in a hurry! All the good times and music coming from outside the bathroom poured in and then shut off when the door closed. Addie was still holding herself and looking past me. I wanted to tell her that me and Georgia was lying.

"Addie," I said, and went to her but she snatched her arm from me. I was scared cause I'd never seen Addie all broke down like that. She was looking how other people looked when she got done with them. "Add." I tried to touch her again, but she wouldn't let me. I started trying to clean up everything then. "We—I don't know what I'm talking bout. Them's just rumors. Folks talking bout what they don't know."

Addie quit looking past me and watched me try to act like everything was light, like I ain't brought no heaviness tween us. I pushed my sweater sleeves over my elbow, crossed my arms, and pulled some kind of tight smile across my face.

"Maybonne." Addie called my name out funny like. "Maybonne, Maybonne. I cain't collect what make me the maddest. That you knowed about Fella and ain't told me nothing, or that you telling me bout it at all . . . Unh." She kept on watching me and I was looking everywhere but where I should of been. In her eyes. "Hm," she say. "I b'lieve what make me the maddest is you telling me now. For yourself. All these years I ain't figured you to be this selfish and evil. Hm," she say again, deciding something, seem like. She straightened herself out, stood as tall as her little short self could, and left me by myself in the bathroom.

I wasn't in there but a second or two after she left cause it gave me a funny feeling, something that went all over me. So I just ran out the bathroom, out Lonnie's, out to the road. Mosely come out after me, asking what was wrong. I hollered at him to leave me alone and ran through the woods. I know every bit of McEwen, every tree, so I didn't have no trouble getting home, though it was black as could be. When I got home, Mama ast me why I'd turned up so early and I told her I was tired. It was a lie and the truth at the same time.

I tried sleeping, tried listening to the radio, but it didn't do no good.

I was still up when Mosely come knocking at the door bout one o'clock in the morning. Had his hat in his hand, looking right strange, not saying a word. He was standing here on this very porch. I say to him, "Addie OK?" thinking that she love that fool Fella so much she might try to hurt herself. But I shoulda knowed better than that. Mosely opened the screen door and come on in. Told me to sit down.

"Baby," he said, "Addie. Addie stabbed Fella down at the café. He tried to get away from her, but she wouldn't let him. Got him twicet. He dead, Maybonne."

Might be hard for you to understand, but I got mad at Mosely then. He was standing there, in my mama's house, talking crazy, telling me Addie'd killed somebody. "You a lie, Mosely!" I hollered and slapped him in the face. He let me do it. Never even tried to stop me.

Mosely sat next to me on the couch and hugged me. He was quiet for a piece before he said, "It's the truth cause I was there. Wisht I wasn't, though. Wisht I wasn't."

And that's all that come from Mosely's mouth bout that night. He wouldn't tell me no more cause he knew it'd hurt me. We just sat there staring out the screen door till Mama told him he'd stayed long enough.

Well, you know it ventually got back to me what Mosely wouldn't tell before. Lot of folks was there and saw Fella's shocked look when Addie come up behind, called his name kind of sweet like, and put that knife in him when he turned around, grinning. He was grabbing his chest, eyes popping out of his head, stumbling through Lonnie's doorway. She jumped on him and stabbed him one more time before folks got sense enough to take the knife from her. But Fella was already dead by the time her mama come and got her out of there.

I ast Mosely if Addie said anything when she was stabbing Fella. Felt like I had to know. Mosely said she just took off her scarf and give it to Sue Baby, this yellow, cross-eyed girl, kind of slow in the head, used to wear them rhinestone cat's-eye glasses all crooked on her face. She told her, "Wipe his face off." And that was it. By the time the police got there, wasn't hardly anybody in Lonnie's but Lonnie—and Fella.

Lonnie's closed down after that cause didn't nobody want to set foot in the place no more. The body was gone and blood had been all scrubbed up, but that thing that was still in the place, well, ain't no cleaning that up. It was haunted, sho nuff.

You can see near bout all of McEwen from this porch, that's how little it is. We ain't never had no murders before then nor since then—come close, though, with all these drunk fools and they shotguns. It ain't like over in Nashville, though, where they just killing each other over them drugs and carrying on.

When Addie killed Fella, her mama packed her up quick and in a hurry! She went to Missouri, and ain't never had to go to jail. Sounds funny, don't it? How you gone to kill a man and not spend a lick of time in jail for it? But that's all the law did. White folks round here then never cared if we killed each other. Just better have sense enough not to mess with em.

A little after all the trouble, I got the number to where Addie was living from her mama. Picked up the phone I don't know how many times, but couldn't never finish dialing them numbers. Before I knowed it, years went by, and then my mama died. At the funeral, I was watching the casket go down into the ground when something told me to look up, and there she was, Addie, standing off to the side and looking at me all calm, like she'd seen me yesterday instead of ten years ago. I'm telling you the truth, the sight of her scared me. My heart jumped into my throat and stayed there. After Mama was laid to rest and folks was leaving, petting on me and telling me they was sorry, Addie started walking towards me, and I started towards her. When we met, we didn't even hug, chile. I think about that. We was talking, but talking like you talk to somebody you don't know, bout the weather, or okra that's only fifty cents a pound down at Green's Market. Stuff that didn't matter. Then she said she had to go, but before she started off, told me to take care. Then, seem like she floated away, walking and walking till she got to the top of that green cemetery hill. *Take care.* Now you hardly got to think to tell somebody that. Anybody and everybody says that to folks.

I'm fixin to tell you something, girl. I hope you never know what it feels like to have that kind of conversation with somebody you knew better than yourself. I hope you don't never know what it is I'm talking bout.

I remember after Addie killed the cat that time, Mama said there was something that wasn't right about her. But you know what? That's everybody, including me and you. It's something that's not right with a lot of folks.

I miss Mosely a lot. He living in Chicago with a wife and kids that treat him right, like they got some kind of sense. Ain't had nobody worth a mention since him, really. He tried to stick with me after that night at Lonnie's, but was all the time talking bout how I'd done changed.

Didn't nobody ever say nothing to my face bout why Addie killed Fella. But folks talk, and I know that little so-and-so Georgia Shields had to go and tell it all bout what was said between me and Addie. Myself, I never told my own mama, not Mosely, not nobody. But the more I tried to get on with things and be happy with Mosely, the more I felt I was doing wrong and trying to get by with it. Felt like any day Mosely was liable to jump up and say, "Girl, what you think you selling me?"

I took to acting like I didn't care whether I had him or not, spending all the time by myself I could, barely speaking to Mosely when I did see him. He finally left me, and I was glad for him, honey. Glad for him.

When Mama died, she left me this house, and I ain't changed it a bit since. I been working down at Ben Franklin's at the cash register for twenty-five years and expect to be there twenty-five more, till they wheel me out in a chair or on a stretcher with a sheet up over my face, honey.

You ain't got to be looking at me like you all sorry, cause you don't know sorry. And I ain't lying when I say this is bout the happiest I'm gone get, sitting out on my porch dipping snuff and watching out over McEwen. Closest to peace I'm gone get.

What I keep looking at? Nothing, I guess. Just thought I saw something over your shoulder. Must be them fireflies, drifting, looking like ghosts. Just like I told you.

hot pepper

I guess nobody thought nothing of Uncle Smiley taking up with that girl because he'd already bought two wives out of a catalogue. Nobody say where the wives be now, but anybody who know anything about Uncle Smiley—that he ain't usually one to be smilin'—know that they prolly got they heels to clicking right about the first time he hit them or stuck the tip of his shotgun in they face. Mama always saying that Uncle Smiley beat his women for breakfast, dinner, and supper. But even so, out of all that, at the time she first turned up it seemed like wasn't nobody worried about Uncle Smiley having the girl up in his house. Now, it ain't but three days later and folks talk about "that poor chile" and about how Uncle Smiley should have been ashamed. I didn't think nothing of it myself—not until he threw her out the house, clothes and everything.

We was skipping rope out in the road in front of Uncle Smiley's house that day. It was me, Jonelle, and our cousin from L.A., Vickie, that be sent down South some summers. We was all taking turns turning the rope when the girl come out on the porch and started watching us. We had a little radio with us, and we was singing along with the song, *Diamond in the back, sunroof top, diggin the scene with a gangsta lean whoo whooo.* I thought for a minute she come out to tell us to quit jumping where we was because every now and then some gravel from the road would fly up over the porch. But she didn't tell us nothing. She never said much, and we never said much to her, even though she was always grinning at us when she saw us playing.

I wanted to turn rope some more because I had put some tissue paper down in the front of my halter top. I wanted to see what I'd look like all filled out like Uncle Smiley's girl, and I was afraid the tissue was going to fall out if I did too much jumping, even though it was my favorite thing to do. My arms was getting tired, though, and Jonelle was complaining that I wasn't turning the rope right and she was messing up because of it.

"Y'all let me turn the rope for you," Uncle Smiley's girl said.

We was all surprised she spoke. "If you wont to," I said.

She come out into the road barefoot like us kids with her toenails painted all bright red. Her halter top looked a lot better on her than mine did on me, and she had on these hot pants that had her behind hanging out of them. She couldn't of been more than four years older than me, but she was looking like I wished I did. I saw how all the boys on the hill was always turning they heads and looking at her and I wished they did me like that.

I handed her my end of the rope and she smiled at me when I took it, but I didn't feel like smiling back. I even sort of cut my eyes at her. I don't know why I did it. But she just kept on grinning.

"Let's do a hot pepper, since you want to jump so bad," the girl said to Jonelle.

A hot pepper is when they turn the rope as fast as they can while you try to keep up. Most of the time if you cain't keep up, that rope slapping your skin burn like hot pepper, too.

She and Vickie started turning the rope fast, and Jonelle was jumping as fast as she could. She never got tangled up in the rope once. I couldn't hardly do hot peppers no more because I wasn't as small as Vickie and Jonelle, but I was thinking of trying to until I remembered the tissue in my halter. Instead I just stood there watching them laugh and clown and carry on. Jonelle got tired after a while, though, and sat down in the middle of the road with all that dust swirling around her.

"Dang. I'm wore out," she said, trying to fan the dust out her way. "You jump," she said to the girl.

"All right. I b'lieve I will jump," the girl said. She handed the rope back to me and was going to start to jump when she saw my cousin, Old Folks, coming up the road.

"Who is that?" she asked, squinting and trying to get a better look at him.

"Oh Lord," Jonelle said. "Here come Old Folks with his slow ass."

Our cousin Old Folks's real name's Nathaniel. He ain't nothing but eighteen, but everybody call him Old Folks because he always move so slow, talk slow, do everything slow. He sweet, though. He sort of liked Uncle Smiley's girl, but the whole three weeks she was with Uncle Smiley, Jonelle and Vickie and them say she never paid no attention to Old Folks until that day. That's what got her in trouble.

Old Folks liked to took all day getting to where we was and sat hisself down on Uncle Smiley's porch. "Whatchall doing?" he said, right slow and all drawled out.

"What it look like?" I said.

"Why you got to be so smart all the time, Bay-Bay?"

I rolled my eyes and put my hands on my hips. I shouldn't of been so mean to Old Folks because I liked him, but I knew he wasn't up on that hill but to see that girl. He hardly ever come round just to talk to us kids. I knew that if my behind was hanging out of my shorts he might of paid more attention to me, though, and it made me mad. I saw him sneaking looks at the girl. She just kept on smiling at him and looking down at those dusty red toenails of hers.

She finally looked Old Folks in the eyes. "You want to jump with us?"

"Ain't that much time in the world," Jonelle said. "What the rope gone do? Wait in the air for Old Folks to jump his slow ass up off the ground?"

We all laughed. Jonelle was younger than me, ten, then come Vickie by a few months, but Jonelle was always cutting up and cussing. She was always saying what was on her mind. Vickie, too, every once in a while, when she got tired of us picking at her and calling her names for not being able to walk around barefoot like the rest of us. But it seemed like it had been a while since I really spoke my mind. Mama said I wasn't no baby no more and I ought to watch what I say to folks and act like a lady.

Uncle Smiley must of heard us laughing and come to his raggedy screen door to see what was going on. I saw him but didn't say nothing, and he didn't speak, either. He just stood there. Nobody else noticed him, and after a while I forgot he was standing there.

"Forget you, Jonelle," Old Folks said, but he was grinning. "You don't want me to show you how it's done. I don't want to show up no little girl."

"Aw, come on," the girl said. "I'll do it with you."

"How I'm gone look, old as I am, jumping rope with y'all?"

She just held out her hand and then waved Old Folks to her.

"Take my end, Vickie," Jonelle said. "My arms is tired."

Me and Vickie was acting stupid with the rope, turning it real slow at first, so slow that Old Folks and the girl could just step over the rope without having to jump. Then we'd try to work in a hot pepper every now and then. Old Folks was a sight. The rope kept slapping his skinny legs after he'd try to jump. He kept getting twisted in the rope with the girl, and we was all laughing and having a good time when Old Folks fell on top of the girl. Thing is, not one of them rushed to get up.

That's when Uncle Smiley opened his screen door. "You chilren is skipping rocks on my porch and I want y'all to go on somewhere else with that rope, you hear? Tammy Lynn, get your tail in this house."

Uncle Smiley was as mad as he could be but didn't look like it. He didn't have no kind of teeth in his mouth and always looked like he was smiling when he wasn't. The corners of his mouth was always turned up, kind of like the mouth carved on a pumpkin. And he had the highest voice in the world. Instead of sounding like the old man he was, he sounded like a little old lady. You wanted to laugh at him, but everybody knew that if you did and he saw you, it was gone be your ass.

"I ain't," the girl said. "We ain't hurting nothing. A few rocks ain't gone hurt your little house."

"Y'all keep turning the rope," she said. "Old Folks?"

"Naw. I b'lieve I'll just watch."

"If you wont to," the girl said, and we started turning the rope for her, even though I was scared of Uncle Smiley. Wasn't that many rocks landing on his porch, but he didn't want us there nohow.

"I ain't gone tell you again, girl," Uncle Smiley said. "You too old to be playing with these kids. Get in this house or I'm gone beat your ass."

"I wish you would," the girl said. "Just because I'm living with you don't mean I'm gone let you run all over me. Your little nasty bed ain't worth all that."

I thought it was gone be all over then. Vickie looked like she was making herself ready to run in case Uncle Smiley went after one of his shotguns, and Jonelle had her hands over her mouth, trying not to laugh. Old Folks was scratching his head, looking everywhere but Uncle Smiley's direction.

Uncle Smiley limped down the porch steps and we all scattered. I never seen Old Folks move that fast before. Uncle Smiley grabbed the girl by her pretty little Afro, drug her up the porch stairs, and tossed her into the house. She was fighting him all the way, too, calling him twenty different kinds of bastards. The screen door slammed behind them. We could hear Uncle Smiley cussing and the girl crying, heard some slaps every now and then. Finally, Uncle Smiley kicked open the screen door and threw a handful a clothes out into the road. Right behind the clothes come Tammy Lynn. Uncle Smiley shoved her down the stairs and she went spilling out into the road.

"But where I'm gone go?" the girl was screaming at Uncle Smiley, but he was inside the house. I couldn't even see him. "I ain't got nowhere to go!"

"It ain't gone be here!" Uncle Smiley called out from inside the house. "Should of thought of that when you was showing out for your boyfriend. You better go on away from here before you be worse off."

The girl was covered with dust, crying like a baby. Her halter top was coming down some and you could see some of her chest. I wanted to do something, just didn't know what. She didn't even look at us nohow. She bundled up all her clothes that was in the road and started walking. Old Folks looked like he was gone go after her, but must of thought on it again, because he looked toward Uncle Smiley's screen door and sat right back down. Then he got up and started walking down the road the opposite direction of the girl.

"That's OK, you old nasty motherfucka!" the girl screamed. She was far enough to be out of Uncle Smiley's slapping range, but close enough for him to still hear her. "I did not like being with you, old man! Why do you think I let you slobber all over me!" Her voice broke on them last words, and it hurt my stomach to hear her that way. We watched her until she got smaller and smaller walking down the road and then I couldn't see her no more.

Me and Jonelle and Vickie just sat in the middle of the road after Tammy Lynn got tossed out, not saying nothing for a while. Then Vickie got up and dusted herself off. "Y'all want to jump some more?" she asked us. Hardly nothing could come between Vickie and playing. I used to be like that, too. Our cousin Shorty fell down one summer when we was playing tag and split her forehead open like a dropped watermelon. I remember we wiped some of the blood off her face with our T-shirts and sent her off to Granny to get stitched so we could finish the game. I didn't think twice about it.

"If we jump," I said, "I'm gone try me a hot pepper."

"You?" Jonelle said. "May as well be Old Folks over here jumping if you gone try it."

"Just watch," I said. But before I started jumping I reached down in my halter and took out all that tissue.

"What you got that for?" Vickie ask me.

"Shut up, Vickie," I said. I didn't feel like explaining nothing to her. She wasn't nothing but a baby. Jonelle was looking at me sly, trying not to grin.

"Let's go," I said. "Get to turning."

We didn't worry about Uncle Smiley coming out the house after us. Even Vickie prolly knew Uncle Smiley didn't whup that girl's behind because of no rocks on his porch.

They tried to turn the rope fast but I jumped rope like they ain't never seen me do. I broke out in a sweat, I was jumping so hard. I didn't mess up once.

Jonelle said I was looking all crazy and mad. Prolly. But it seem like, as hard as I was jumping rope, doing them hot peppers, my heart just wasn't in it.

clay's thinking

Trip out. She's not the type that usually scams on me. All professional. But this one's trying to. She looks like she works in an office with her suit-type thing going on, gold jewelry, all that. I'll have to investigate what's up with her. First time I see her, I'm in the photo lab, wearing my pussy uniform and developing the usual lame pictures when she comes through the door. She's got a camera in her hand like she wants it fixed or something, and she just rolls up to me and asks me about the skull tattooed on my bicep. She says it's cool. But it's not even finished yet. The flames shooting out of the eye sockets and mouth ain't even colored in yet. I'ma get it done in yellow and red. It's gonna be bad.

Right off, though, I'm thinking she's cool even if she has her little office thing going on. Usually my tats keep the people away that need to be kept away, and if people don't look at me like I'm a fucking criminal and shit then I know they're cool people. If you're freaked-out by my tats, then step off. You don't need to be knowing me. This girl, she wasn't like that. She was cool. She did want her camera fixed, though, and was holding it up to me, like I'm mister technology guy, like I know how to fix a camera. I'm all, "I'm sorry, but I just develop the film and stuff." She goes, "Oh," and gives me this little smile like, "Duh, I'm such a moron." It was cool. Most people would be all up in my face, pissed at me cause I'm not the one to fix their shit. She just stood there, and then she goes, "Well, thank you anyway." I stare at her, I'm all, "Uh, you're welcome." Trevor's all, "I can help you over here, miss." She bailed after tight-ass Trevor helped her out.

She keeps coming in for small things, kind of lame stuff. I know what's up. She asked if she could touch my bat tattoo the other day. I'm outside on my lunch break, eating my burger when she walks by. I had my shirt off cause I was roasting, no shit. It was Africa hot. I could see her coming up the street, and she could see me, but I didn't wave at her cause she wasn't close enough yet. I would have looked all retarded waving at her when she's way down the block and shit. When she got up to me, she was looking at my chest and every-thing before she looked me in the eyes. I lift every day and I'm cut, so I know she was checking out my stuff. She's all, "That bat's neat. It didn't hurt you to get it on your shoulder blade like that? You mind?" And then she runs her fingers over it. When she did that, my stom-ach got all crazy on me but I played it off. I just kept chewing my food.

She told me her name was Mirabella. Classy sounding, huh? All the chicks I know are named Lisa or Kim, or like, Shauna. I swear to God. She sat next to me on the bench while I was eating and we watched all the psychos and tight-asses in their suits walk by. She was asking me all these questions, like where I'm from and stuff. I could tell we were the same age, even if she did talk kind of old. But that's probably cause she works in an office and's got to be all proper and shit.

I had to get back to the dumb film or else Trevor wouldn't let me bail early for practice. My band, Black Company, we're trying to get our shit together. When I tell her I got practice tonight, she gets all impressed. She goes, "I thought you might be a musician. That's wonderful." I start laughing and she looks at me serious. She goes, "What?"

I go, "Nothing." But she said *wonderful.* That shit was funny.

I should of been getting back inside, but she was vibing me *hard.* Playing with her hair and looking me up and down. I never had that before. Usually I gotta work hard to get some play and that barely works cause I don't know what the fuck I'm doing. But she was making it easy. So I ask her to come to our gig Friday night. She goes, "Cool," but it sounded kind of funky when she said it, like if somebody's moms was saying it. Cute, though. I tell her, "So, see you Friday maybe."

She waits for me to open the door to the store, and then she goes, "Clay." So I turn around. Then she says, "I like you." Like that. Crazy girl.

The bat Mirabella was touching is flying over a red heart and the fangs are like, digging into it. My old girlfriend's name, Lisa, used to be in the heart, but she played me and took off with some guy.

Before that, my girl, Sandy, started creeping with Javier, this dude I used to be cool with. I found him and fucked him up real bad. I still have Sandy tattooed down the side of my calf, but just cause it's my mom's name, too. But the day after Lisa left me? I had Albert at the tat joint cover that bitch's name with the bat. My mom said, "Clay, I told you." But I told her to leave me alone. She hates tattoos because my dad got a bunch of them right after he went to jail again, this time for jacking some guy that tried to talk smack. And when he got out, she never heard from him again. That's what she told me.

I barely remember my dad, just that he called me Pellet because I'm short with a thick neck, just like him. My mom doesn't even have a picture of him around the house or anything. But it's cool. She says *I'm* his picture, right down to the crazy slanted green eyes. The craziest looking Irishman she'd even seen. When I got my first tat I was thinking of me and my dad, both of us bleeding and getting injected with dye, being connected that way. My mom says that's just like me and just like him to think up something stupid like that. Like twins.

Mirabella turns up at the gig looking *hot*. She's got this curly big hair, black like a crow. It's all over the place. She looks crazy luscious, wearing this cootchie cutter skirt. *Damn.* I introduce her to my buds and they act all polite. They got *manners* all of a sudden, so I know they dig her. I'm working her too, best behavior, all that. Some drunk fucker tries to start some shit just before our set, screaming we sucked or whatever, because we only do Ramones and Dead Kennedys covers. We're going to start writing our own songs, though, stupid motherfucker. If Mirabella wasn't there, man, I swear to God. But I kicked back. I go up to the dude and I'm all, "Sir, if you don't calm down I'm going to have to get some security happening over here." He tripped cause he was like, seventeen, and I called his dumb ass "Sir." He sat the fuck down.

Mirabella stares at me the whole time so I show off, doing the rock star thing. We only played five songs, then some other shitty band had to go on. After the gig, Mirabella comes up to me and kisses me, just like, no bullshit. She asks me if I want to go to her house for a drink. Check her out. A *drink*. I say yeah, thinking *hell* yeah, but I'm tripping cause all this shit's on me. She's telling me something and I don't want to punk out and fuck it up. I grab my guitar and tell everybody to deal with the stack of Marshalls and the rest of the stuff. My bass player Eric, he's pissed but when I tell him Mirabella's taking me to her house, he goes, "Right on, Bro. You grabbing her or what?" All loud. What a dick. I don't think she heard him, though.

We go out to the parking lot, and her car's one of those girlie red Miatas. Kind of embarrassing. I'm standing there looking at it. But I can't say shit, cause I got no car, no license. I used to have a 427 Chevy with dual holleys, but I got fucked-up one night, herb, beer, all that. I flipped it, trashed it. I got busted and had to wear one of those lame orange vests and pick up shit along the freeway for community service. I made my moms cry behind all that shit, too. I don't know what's up with me half the time. Anyways, I get in the Miata and tell Mirabella it's a cool car.

"You don't have to lie," she says. "I saw the way you were looking at it." And I just look at her cause I can't believe she cold busted me like that. It's her cousin's car, she says. He died and left it to her. Crazy. What the hell am I supposed to say about sad stuff like that?

When we get on the freeway, I see what a fucked-up driver she is. She's looking at me while she's talking to me, like we're sitting across from each other at a fucking table, I swear to God. I don't want to die in no piece-of-shit aluminum Miata, so I go, "Babe, you can't be driving and looking at me at the same time." She just laughs and says, "I like that. Babe," and keeps driving like she ain't heard me, crazy girl.

We drive all through Mulholland before we get to her crib, one of those crazy houses with glass for walls and shit. When we get out the car, I reach for my guitar in the backseat. Mirabella tells me not to worry about somebody snaking it, she says to leave it, and I'm all, "Yeah, right, you must be high," and take my ax with me. I follow her up some stairs and I'm checking out her ass, like *inches* from my face, when I fall into her cause she's stopped at the door to open it.

She looks over her shoulder and goes, "You OK?" She's got an ass like BAM! A *shelf*, man. I don't say jack cause I'm feeling all dumb. But I kind of hold her ass in my hands. She just winks at me.

The vibe's weird inside her crib. She's got some funky kind of light going on, like at the museum. All like, *dramatic*. Furniture coordinated and shit. Slick wood floors, fucking shiny, man. Wet looking. I'm just standing there holding onto my guitar. I don't even want to *move*. I'm about to tell her let's just go out to the car, check out the stars or whatever, but she's already walking down this long hallway, asking me what I want to drink. I'm tripping cause my boots sound loud, like I'm stomping and shit, but I'm trying to walk all soft. "Mira, don't you have no carpet in this joint?" I'm just being stupid, trying to make myself feel normal. But then my case knocks over this big curly, haunted-house-looking candleholder thing, taller than me. I mean it fucking crashes on the floor. Mirabella comes running with a wine bottle in her hand and when she sees me standing there looking like I'm going to jail, she starts cracking up. She's all, "What are you *doing*?"

I go, "What's up with this Dracula shit? This shit's dangerous." I pick it up and rub my palms on my jeans cause I'm nervous. There's this big-ass red mark on the wall from one of the candles. She's laughing, though. My moms would have been screaming like Manson was knifing her. I'm totally digging this girl.

I follow her into the kitchen. It looks fake, like she don't cook in it, like at the furniture store. You know how they always got the little living rooms and kitchens and stuff and there's always some fucked-up looking plastic fruit in a bowl on the counter? Like that.

She's waving the wine bottle around, asking me if I want some. I can't stand wine. It's *seriously* nasty. I don't see how people can drink it. I ask for a beer and she's cool about it. We're sitting at the little bar in the kitchen for a while, and then I remember the bud and pipe in my jacket. Mirabella wants some herb, too, so we puff some and start to get buzzed. I can't even stop looking at her. She looks way good. She's leaning over the bar laughing and going on and on about the gig, how she liked watching me play. She's all talking about the way the veins in my arms stick out when I play and that I look sexy all sweaty with my eyes closed.

I go, "How dumb." But in my head, I'm going, Clay dude, you want some of that. I want to be this chick's man for real. I start jonesing for her real bad, and I'm about to tell her when we hear somebody coming through the door. I jump up, looking for a way to jam out of there, wondering what to do with my bud. I'm scared. I don't care if I look like a punk, either. But then Mirabella just goes, "Hank?" all smooth and chill.

"Yep," this guy goes. I hear him walking down the hall and then he's standing there looking at us. He's like this old dude, like forty, dressed all pimp sharp and shit. Silk shirt and creased pants. Hair slicked back with gray streaks in it.

I'm tripping for real now. I don't know *what's* up. And Mirabella walks up to him and kisses him. She goes, "Hey, baby. What are you doing home?" I'm like, hold up. *Baby* and *home?* Fuck me. I'm feeling like twenty different kinds of jackasses.

This dude says his flight was canceled or something, but he's hardly paying attention to me, like it's not weird that I'm in his house with his woman. Mirabella goes, "Clay, Hank. Hank, Clay. You know my friend I told you about?" He looks tired or something, and he holds out his hand like he's doing something he don't even want to do. But I'm like, *whatever*. I'm not shaking grandpa's hand. I just nod at him.

I tell her, "Look. I gotta go." I grab my guitar and start stomping down her dumb-ass shiny fucking floor, like I'm going somewhere, but she's got to take me home. I gotta get in that fucking Miata again and be driven home by some other dude's woman like a pussy. I'm in a way fucked-up situation. Mirabella comes after me, she's looking all sad or whatever, so I go on down the stairs and get in the car. She starts talking to me. She's sorry, she was gonna tell me what was up, she should have told me earlier, blah blah. Yeah, shoulda coulda woulda. I turn my head and put my hand in her face. This corny thing I saw on TV just kind of came to me, so I'm all, "Save the drama for your mama."

She looks shocked, eyes all big and mouth hanging open like I backhanded her. I'm kind of sorry I said it, though. She puts her hands on the steering wheel for a minute and then takes them off. She moves closer to me. Then she puts her hand on my knee. "Clay, please," she says. Soft, almost a whisper. No chick's begged me before. It was kind of cool. She leans into me and rubs her face against mine. Soft, man. And she smells all kinds of good.

I go, "Mirabella, you played me. That's so wack." I'm supposed to be sounding hard but she's got me whispering. She goes, "Let me tell Hank that your girlfriend can't come and get you, so you need a ride." She's all pulling up my shirt and junk, rubbing my belly, saying, "Please," kissing me on the tip of my ear. I know this girl's used to getting everything she wants. But I'm not even thinking about Mr. GQ upstairs. Fuck him if he can't keep his woman off some other dude's jock. Maybe I got too crazy on Mirabella, I'm thinking. Overacted or whatever. I'm thinking me and her could go places.

And we do.

I call her up a lot, tell her to come over. She does, even if it's some crazy time in the morning. I dig living with Eric, because Mirabella can swing by whenever. Eric and Felis don't care. Only this one time I got Mirabella going real good. She made all kinds of noise, moaning and hollering like I was killing her instead of doing her. I went downstairs to get her some water after, and Eric was all, "Bro, take it easy up there, man. Felis was trying to get the kid to go to sleep." I go, "Sorry," and he laughed at me. He goes, "What a piece of ass, man. What the fuck she doing with you?" He was just fucking with me, but after that, whenever Mira came over I tried to make her scream real loud, especially my name.

I'm always thinking about her. I'll just be in my room, lying on my bed staring at the ceiling, thinking about how her hair would be all in my face, in my nose and eyes and mouth if she was in the bed with me. When she's here, that girl's got my whole room smelling like her. She washes her hair with some herbal shit that gets all over the place. Last time I told her that, we were on the floor messing around. She said the room just smelled like smoke to her.

I go, "Whatever. *Mother.* You want me to quit?" My moms is always sweating me about my smokes. She's always saying, "Clay, they'll kill you. You want that?" One time I said, "Maybe." She smacked me. But later she said she was sorry. She was puffing on a Camel. My moms. Man.

She finally kicked me out cause I kept fucking-up—partying, smoking too much bud, getting my ass thrown in jail. First, I thought it was cold how she kicked me to the curb like that. She'd call around checking on me where she figured I crashed, wanted to talk to me. I was like, *whatever*. What she want to know? How fucked-up it feels to be dissed by your own mother? I blew her off for a long time, too. That's how I got my dumb-ass job at the photo shop and ended up living with Eric and his lady, Felis. I had to stop fucking around then and take care of myself. For a long time I thought my moms put me in a fucked-up situation, but we're cool now. I get it.

Mirabella said she didn't want me to quit smoking because I looked sexy when I smoked. She said I squinted and looked out the corner of my eye, or some shit like that. I got in this fucked-up mood after that. She climbed on me and kissed me, unbuttoned my jeans and had her hand all on my stuff. But I was tripping, not feeling anything. She was acting all hurt cause I wasn't into it. She was kissing me on the neck, biting me like I like, but I shined her.

"What would you do if I like, got lung cancer and shit and died from trying to look all sexy. What would you do then, huh?"

She was still kissing my neck. She's all, "You. You will never ever *ever* die, Clayton Bailey." I swear when she said it I was believing her. That kissing on my neck was starting to get to me, even if I was still feeling fucked-up.

"What do you tell your man when you're with me? He don't ask questions?"

"What? Where did that come from?"

I stared at her cause I just didn't feel like answering her.

She finally says, "Oh, a lot of different things." She like, whispers in my ear, trying to sound all sexy. "I say I'm out with a friend." She puts the tip of her tongue in my ear and it sort of tickles so I tell her to knock it off.

"Like me? He's cool with that?" I'm chewing on my nails. I do it all the time without even thinking about it. I spit one of the nails out and stare at the ceiling.

She grabs my hand and kisses all the fingers. "Don't. You have such beautiful hands." She checks out my nails. "You shouldn't bite them." And then she rubs her face with my hand. "I have a lot of friends, Clay. It's not unusual, my being out with friends. Hank has friends, too."

All that sounded way out fucked-up to me, but I let it go. Felt like some shit I didn't want to know. I'm all, "So where are they, these friends? Bring em to my gigs so we can party."

"I only got time for you, baby," she says. She pokes me in the side and kind of winks both eyes really hard, like my little cousin Kenny. He don't know how to do it yet. I like how she can be goofy sometimes. Normal, like everybody else. I play fake rough with her and hold her arms behind her back so I can look at her good. She's breathing all heavy, waiting for me to do something. I can tell she likes it.

I go, "Hey, monkey face. You're so ugly, you got no friends." I tickle her under her arms till she can't even breathe anymore. She's laughing and screaming, "I do have friends, Clay! I have pictures to prove it!"

She likes to take pictures. I've seen a lot of them, mostly freaky-looking, like a stick with a glass of milk next to it. Black-and-white stuff. Mira had her camera out, taking pictures of me naked, crawling on her knees and stuff like those fruity guys that photograph models. "God, I wish I could do this all day," she says.

I go, "Do what? Scope my hot bod?"

She takes the camera away from her face so I can see her roll her eyes. But then she smiles at me.

"Pictures, Clay. Pictures." She puts the camera back up to her face and starts with her acrobatic shit again. I sit up in bed but she yells at me to get back in the sunlight.

"So take pictures all day. Quit that office gig. Grandpa's got bucks."

"Don't call him that." She stops taking pictures and sits down on the floor next to the bed. I'm staring at the back of her head. She don't answer me, so I thump her on the head. I go, "Hey. You know you don't have to work."

She stands up and climbs on me, holds my hand back like we're wrestling. If I barely coughed, I'd knock her off, but I let her hold me down. She gets in my face and makes our noses touch. She goes, "Then I'd really be stuck. In his house and everything."

"I might want to be be stuck like that," I tell her. "In that big-ass rich house?"

"No you don't."

"So move out of what's-his-face's house and get your own crib."

"Stuck some more. In that job." She kisses me all over my face, then she sits up straight and takes off her shirt. She was wearing this lace bra thing with a trippy pattern on it. Zig zaggy and curly and shit. For me, she says.

"What's wrong with your bra?" I say, fucking with her. "It hurts my goddamn eyes, girl."

She goes, "Shut up, Clay," and bites my chin like a psycho. I go "Ow!" even though it didn't hurt. "Do you think I'm pretty?" she asks me, and I'm looking at that crazy hair of hers, her skin that's like the color of almonds, gold eyes, and these insane lips she has, that are like fucking magnets for my eyes. I can't stop looking at them.

She knows what I think, so I go, "You're aw-ight. What about me, do you think I'm pretty?" And we both start rolling cause I sound like the fruitiest motherfucker you've ever heard in your life. Mira's snorting, she's laughing so hard, and she's so fucking fine she can get away with that shit.

Every piece-of-shit hole in the wall we play at, she's there. Taking picture like we're the biggest band on the planet. None of my girls ever did that for me. I mean she's all up on the stage practically, camera flashing. Makes me feel like I'm the M.A.N.

Last night we played at some freaky place I don't even remember. But the people were like fucking mummies, I swear to God. I played like it wasn't no big thing, but I was pissed. Later I told Eric I ain't never playing there again, they can kiss my ass. Mirabella was there drunk. This *sexy* girl Candace, some girl from her job, was with her. My buddy Danny was all on that shit because we found out she stripped, so he thought he could get some easy. She was so out of his league, it wasn't even funny. Anyway, we found out she had a man, so Danny stopped sweating her.

I trip on Mirabella sometimes because when she's downtown she looks all businessy or whatever, all serious. But when she comes to the gigs she's wild, like it's the only time she has fun. Starving for it or something. Her girl Candace left Mira at the gig early because her man was paging her. So Mira stayed and got fucked-up on some of that nasty champagne she drinks all the time and started screaming for the people to get off their asses. She starts dancing around, bumps into some chick. Then the chick gets mad and the two of them start rolling around. Flashing their underwear. People were yelling, "Cat fight, right on!" It was kind of funny at first, but then that chick scratches Mirabella's face real bad and she starts crying.

Eric's like, "Bro, you better check your girl," so I take off my guitar and jump down in between them to break it up and the two of them fuck *me* up. I *still* got scratches on my neck trying to referee. I pull her outside to give her some air and check her out. I'm asking if she's cool and everything. She's got these little pink stripes across her cheek from where that chick scratched the shit out of her. Mirabella goes off on me, though.

"Leave me alone!" She pushes me, and then crosses her arms and stands in front of me like little kids do when they're throwing their little tantrums or whatever. I'm just standing there with my fucking mouth wide open. Tripping.

Finally, I go, "What's up with you? What did I do?"

Her eyes were practically closed. She was way liquored. "I don't needs to be cared and taken care of, Clay! I got my own mine." She couldn't even talk right. Her words were coming out all fucked-up. I think she was talking about having her own mind. Something. She points at me and goes, "You understand?"

I started rubbing the stubs of my hair. Eric shaved my head cause we were bored after we got stoned one night. When she first saw it, Mira said I looked cool, like I just got out of prison.

"Baby, you're talking out your ass." I grab her wrist and pull her to me. I hold her hand in mine. Girls have funny little hands. I was running the tips of my fingers over her skin. She always digs that. But she starts crying again. Her makeup was running down her face, making these black lines. She still looked good, though.

She put her face in my chest and cried all over my T-shirt. I wrapped my arms around her and put my chin in her hair. She smelled so good. That herbal shit she uses. I swear, man. I wanted her bad. She goes, "You're lucky, Clay," and some other stuff I couldn't hear because she was talking into my shirt. Then she ran over to this palm tree and threw up. I stood behind her and pulled her crazy hair out of the way so she wouldn't get any barf in it. I rubbed her back while she was throwing up and everything. I felt bad. I go, "Let it out, Mira, let it out," until she was just heaving and not throwing up anymore.

I develop all of Mira's pictures for free. She shouldn't have to pay for pictures of my dick, or spit on the sidewalk, or whatever crazy thing she says is art. I'm checking out all the pics to make sure I didn't fuck em up somehow, and I notice this picture of me talking to April, this skank chick that's always trying to jock me. Her mouth's wide open, and she's holding her hands way out apart from each other like she's measuring something, and way in the background, in the doorway of the joint, there's Mirabella's fucking boyfriend. Right there. I only saw him that one time but I'd know his old rico suave silk-shirt-wearing ass for sure. I start to call Mirabella at work and ask her about it, see if she knew he was there, but I wait until she stops by on her lunch break. I don't say anything. I want to know what she's got to say about it. I just put the picture out there on top of the glass case where we keep all the lenses and stuff we sell. She picks it up by the edges so she won't get fingerprints on it, and then she scrunches her nose like something stinks. "This isn't a good photograph at all. Man, I must have been *extremely* inebriated when I took this."

I hate it when she talks all that photography stuff I don't know. Just cause I work in a lab she thinks I know what the fuck she's talking about. I tell her, "Maybe you were drunk or something," and she just laughs for no reason. She always does that. She can't see what's-his-face in the picture, so I point to him.

She makes this weird squeaky kind of noise and puts her hand over her mouth. I go, "Mira, are you cool?" but she won't say anything. Trevor looks up from the register. He's all, "Clay, is she all right?" I don't know, so I don't say anything. I walk her outside and sit her down. After a long time watching the traffic, she says, "Maybe we spend too much time together."

I shouldn't of showed her that shit. I should of torn it up and thrown it in the trash.

She takes me home after work, and we're hanging in my room, talking, playing around. I asked her to go down on me and she did, like always. All I gotta do is ask and she'll do it, any kind of sex I want. But I'm whipped, too. I'm not even going to front like I ain't. But this time, after we fool around, I really wanted her to stay. I always want her to stay, but this time I really did. I ask her to spend the night. Sometimes she can, when her man's not in town, but when he's in town, she's gotta hop to. I could tell she didn't want to stay because she was freaked-out by the picture.

I'm watching her put her blue suit and jewelry on, wondering what it would be like to watch her get dressed for work every morning. If we lived together, I could ask her stupid stuff like, "Mirabella, where's my brown belt with the silver buckle?" Or "Baby, did you wash my shirt? I can't find it." Like that. I was just thinking about how cool that would be.

I go, "Mirabella. Just stay, man. I want you to." She keeps getting dressed like she ain't heard me. I'm lying in my bed naked, but I get up when she doesn't answer me. I'm standing behind her, watching her fix herself up in the mirror. I wrap my arms around her and kiss her neck. I'm thinking, if I can get her going again she won't bail on me. But she just sort of pulls away from me and goes, "Come on, Clay. Really. I have to go." She's walking away from me so I grab her wrist. I take her hand and put it on me. I'm not even hard, but I want her to know I can go again. But she yanks her hand away like I put it on a fire or something. She's all, "Knock it off." Cold just like that. She had me standing there looking stupid.

I walk to her real slow. I'm all up in her face. I go, "What's your problem? Why you talking to me like I'm crazy?" She looks like she's kind of scared for a sec, cause I never did that before, get in her face. But then her eyes get that soft look they do when I know for sure she gives a shit about me and I know for sure that she *knows* me. She rubs my chin, but I'm still pissed. I take her hand off my face and hold it real tight in case she tries to get away from me again. I ask her, "What's he got that I don't? I'm tired of you leaving me for him." I swear to God, I didn't even know I was going to say that. I kind of felt like a pussy.

She goes, "Clay, you know I have to get home. You saw the picture."

"Fuck the picture." I pull her to me and hold her face in my hands. "You go home, pack your shit, jam outta there. Stay here with me in my room."

She looks around the room. Then she goes, "It's not easy like that, Clay."

I feel like being a dick to her, so I go, "Just cause I can't buy you a new car like grandpa. Next time, let him make you come."

I could tell she was going to cry cause she turned her back to me, but when I tried to talk to her again she ran out. When I heard her drive away, I felt like putting my fist through the fucking wall. I called down to Eric and asked him if he wanted to get high with me, but he didn't.

The next day, Mirabella comes to the photo shop asking to see me. I tell her I can't take a break, that Trevor's been riding my ass all day. I'm totally lying, but I just can't deal with her big brown eyes, the smell of her, her beautiful ass. She goes, "I see. Perhaps later," talking her office talk.

She turns around to go, and I'm going to let her, too. She gets to the door and I gotta open my big mouth. I can't stand to see her walking away. I'm all, "Hey." She turns around and crosses her arm, doing that tantrum thing. I go, "We got a gig tonight, girl. In Hollywood. Nine-thirty." She grins at me, all happy. Usually when I see that, it makes *me* happy. But I was bummin all of a sudden.

At the gig Mirabella was taking pictures of me playing. It was bothering me for some reason. Shit didn't feel the same. Like, I was feeling like . . . like if you can't even *be* with me, be with me, like anytime you want, then what's with a *picture* of me? I got this vibe like I was her school project or something, like she was making a memory of my ass, and if you're already a *memory* of some chick before she's even told you anything about what's up with you and her, I don't know. You know what I'm saying? I told her, "Look, Mirabella, I don't want you taking pictures of me playing, I can't concentrate."

She's all, "What are you talking about? You said you loved it."

I go, "That was then. I don't anymore, all right?"

You know what that crazy bitch did? She threw her camera on the floor. A fucking top-of-the-line Nikon. Trashed it. She's all, "You don't want pictures? Fine." She kicked the camera across the room like a psycho. Crazy girl.

She came home with me, though. After the gig. She wanted to stay because her man was out of town. I told her I felt sick, that she shouldn't stay. Maybe I wasn't sick, but I felt messed up anyway. She looked at me all weird but she left. Didn't even ask me if I needed anything before she left. I know I'm tripping, cause I wasn't really sick. But still. She could of asked.

Trevor found out I was developing all of my friends' pictures for free. Mostly Mirabella's. So what? He calls me into his office in the back of the store and then tells me to shut the door.

He's sitting behind his shitty Kmart-looking desk shuffling his two papers. Then he starts in, sounding like he memorized that shit. "Clay, it has come to our attention that you have been developing photographs for free, which is against store policy." That's what he said to me. I just stood there staring at him with my hands in my pockets, wishing I had a cigarette. He waited for a little bit, like I was supposed to say something. But I was staring at his neck, a fucking pencil, I swear to God.

"Clay?" he says, all patient like a damn doctor or something. I fucking hate Trevor. He was looking at me and blinking his watery eyes.

I go, "Trev, everybody that works here does that shit. What are you calling me in here for?" I still had work to do before I bailed for the day, a bunch of film for this attorney who was always coming in for his stuff like two hours before I told his ass. It was always pictures of the same big-headed baby in the same pose in every single picture.

Trevor stood up and put his hands in his pockets. He was sweating. *This motherfucker is firing me.* I finally got it.

He says, "We're going to have to let you go, Clay," but I barely heard him. I didn't say nothing, because I was thinking about how I was going to beat the shit out of his skinny Lurch ass.

I step to him and tell him, "You punk-ass motherfucker, what kind of shit is this? That ain't no reason." He yells for Mike, the other developer, then. Like he's going to do something.

Mike busts in all dramatic, fucking Superman. He goes, "Dude, just go, all right?" and then he stands next to Trevor, like that's supposed to scare me. I was so pissed, before I left I picked up the chair I was standing next to and threw it at their sorry asses. One of the legs tagged Mike right on his fucked-up peanut-looking forehead, but I don't think I hurt him bad. I was almost out of the store when I heard Trevor yell something like, "Maybe you should have tried coming to work not fucked-up on herb, too!" Motherfucker. I only came to work high a couple of times.

Mira can calm me down when I'm wired, make me feel better. It's the way she says my name and plays with my hair. Since I shaved my head, she rubs it and says she's making wishes. I feel like if I don't see her right now I'm going back to the lab and beat the shit out of Trevor. I've been to Mirabella's office before on the weekend, but everybody worked in these sections that were put together like a fucking maze, so I couldn't find her right away. I was feeling kind of tight walking through there. Uncomfortable or whatever. Two people asked me if I was from some place—Professional Express, they called it. They thought I was delivering something. When I said I was looking for Mirabella, their eyes got big like I said I was looking for Santa Claus or some shit.

I found her talking with this white-haired guy in a suit, just like all the other tight-asses. She's all these accountant dudes' administrative assistant. Something like that. This guy was all in her face, laughing and being Mr. Smooth. I stood there until she saw me, and she goes, "Clay!" like she was busted for something. The two of them stood there staring at me, until I go, "Mira, can I talk to you? For like, two seconds?" But then the freak she was talking to doesn't even move until she says, "It's OK."

I mad-dog the guy while he's walking away. I go, "What's up with *that*? You got two grandpas now or what?" I put my hands on her waist and pull her to me. I need a kiss from this girl. I want her to put her arms around me. But she holds back.

"I told you not to call Hank that, Clay. Richard just didn't know you, that's all." She starts playing with this gold necklace she's wearing.

I step back and look at her. "Who the hell is he supposed to be that he's got to know me?"

She starts adjusting a pin in her hair. She's got it up in a bun. I hate it that way. Finally she goes, "What's the matter, Clay? Why are you here?" So I tell her how I got screwed. She doesn't even look surprised, but she takes my hand and squeezes it. "I'm sorry," she tells me. I try to hug her again, but she sits down on her desk and looks around to see if anybody's watching.

She's all, "Not at my work, Clay." When she says that, I want to smack her. I want to remind her of the time I did her right there on her dumb-ass important desk.

"You know what?" I tell her. I can't wait to get out of there. "You're fucked." When I turn around to bail, she grabs me by my shirt and tells me to wait, so I do. She wants to say something, I can tell. I'm waiting. She lets go of my shirt and just stands there, looking at me. So I break out. I go catch my fucking bus.

Nobody's around when I get home. The whole neighborhood's quiet—kids in school, everybody at work. All I can hear are birds talking every once in a while. Makes me feel fucked-up, like I wish somebody was around with me to talk shit to or smoke a joint with. So I light a joint and kick back. I start thinking about how I don't have a damn job anymore. Eric and Felis won't let me stay in their crib for free if I ain't working. I'm going to have to go back crawling to my mom's house, begging for a place to stay. She's going to start in, make me feel shitty, like a five-year-old.

And you know what? I'm sitting here thinking: I don't even have one single picture of Mirabella. Like if I wanted to show somebody, "Look, dude. I used to be with this girl. I used to be this girl's man," I can't do it. I developed a shitload of pictures of myself for her, and I didn't even *think* about wanting a picture of her the whole time I was working in the lab. I just wanted to get to her and be with her. And now I don't even have a fucking negative.

bars

You tell me: a woman in a bar, all alone. *Hopping* bars all alone. What you think about that? See? I knew you'd say that: what she looking for in a bar all by herself? You sound like my son Rasheed, or La Trice, my daughter, trying to tell me like you know so much. But what I'm telling you is yeah, that's right. I like bars. I like going to bars alone. And it ain't got to be all about me looking for something. If a man got a right to sit here on a stool, have a drink, talk to the bartender, why can't I do it? Ain't about looking for something.

My daughter always trying to tell me what I should and shouldn't do. I feel like I got two mamas! "*Mother*," she says (and where "mother" come from when it been "mama" for I don't know how long?) "a woman going to a bar alone is *desperate*." I don't know who she thought she was talking to, and I had to ask her who she was calling desperate. She rolled her eyes then, cause the child know she too old for me to whup her behind. But let me tell you something: that girl don't wear underwear! Trying to call *me* desperate! Be wearing dresses you can see right through and ain't got no draws on! She *say* she got a thong on sometimes. One time I said, "Let me see." She showed me, and *honey*. I said, "Them's stripper panties, ain't they?" I just didn't know *what* in the world.

"Mother," she says again. And I just shut up about it cause she grown and if she don't know by twenty-six years old that you triflin if you can't find no draws to put on, I ain't got nothing else to do with it.

Look at this brother sitting two stools down. You just know my man had him a bad day. Sitting on his jacket, sleeves rolled up, tie loose. Just all tore down. Make me want to say, "Damn. Have a drink on *me*." But then he'd probably try to get smooth on me, and I ain't come here for that.

Sometimes it's cool to just go inside a dark place while it's still light outside. And I do that a lot. They know me here at The Gaelic and a couple other places, too. This place is nice, though. Supposed to be Irish-like. They got the plaid everywhere, but they also hung up some moose heads and horns and stuff, which kind of confuses the theme, to me.

But you come in here, and it's dark, red leather booths, dart game going on in the corner usually. Rickie part owns the place. She's always in here wearing her tight jeans and some earrings that match the holiday. Like the pumpkins she's wearing now. But it ain't Halloween. It's Easter. So maybe Rickie just likes pumpkins. Rickie does look hard, like a woman who spends a lot of time in a bar might look, just like my mama claims going to happen to me. But me and Rickie two different people. I'm forty and got a long road before I'll be catching up with Rickie. Rickie's got some serious lines in her face. Not saying nothing bad about Rickie, I'm just saying.

Here she comes now.

"Hey, Doll!" She always says that. "What's new?" Staring at me with big gray eyes blinking lashes with about three coats of mascara. She's got them looking like fake lashes but they hers, I can tell. And Rickie ain't going nowhere until I say, "Can't complain" or "Fine." Answer her *something*. Then she goes on with her white-boot-wearing self. Rickie still looking good, though. Shoot. Ain't nothing wrong with Rickie.

Just don't get me started on the man she run with. Treat her any which way. Like last night, I'm sitting here, trying to talk to this rough-cut, quiet man that said he sold car parts for a living. So we was chatting when Rickie's man Pete came through the door with an old papery-looking, washed-out blonde hanging on him. Didn't look like no friend of the family. The way conversations drop and the music seemed to get louder, I know the regulars made the same observation I did. Now, Rickie's man Pete, he's just a dried-up little man himself, compliment Old Papery, really. Rickie should have told him not to let the knob hit him on the back on his way out. But she cussed and carried on over Pete. Chased the woman out, but kept Pete. That's how a woman'll do. Get in the other woman's face but keep the man. We'll stick with what we know, cause what we don't know is worse. Most of the time.

Me and my kid's father, we separated ten years ago when Rasheed was five, but he takes care of his son. He's a good man. For some other woman, not me. We don't have much to say to each other. Cause he's crazy. I guess I'm part crazy, too, and we liked to drive each other crazy. But that's where Rasheed got his computer that can do anything and everything. Not like that old stuff they got us on at the phone company. Anyway, it's messing around on Rasheed's computer that got me mixed up in stuff so crazy, I practically ran over folks to get in here and wash all the junk down with a drink. Some drinks.

So Rasheed gets this computer, and when he gets tired of it he wants to teach me some stuff. Talked to me like I was the child, called himself giving me a lesson. Finally, I had to say, "Look. Your mama ain't slow. I know what I'm doing." You only got to tell me once how to do something. Then I'll be giving you lessons!

I was on Rasheed's computer, on the line, online, I mean, checking the little areas here and there. Rasheed wanted me to research how much it cost to take a safari in Africa. Whatever it cost he ain't got it. I said, "Boy, you better fly to Oakland and be happy with that." He didn't think that was funny. I found him some prices (they talking about three thousand dollars!), got tired of that, so I said, let me go into one of these rooms, these chat rooms. I want to know what everybody's chatting about, see. I start reading the lists, trying to pick a room, and *honey*. They got something for everybody. I can't remember what all I saw, but I went from chess players to married-but-looking to vampires to witches before I said, hold up. Let me go back to the beginning of the list, start early in the alphabet and get away from these freaks.

Before I go on, I need Rickie to hook me up with another Bloody Mary. Just my second and my last now. Not like it's your business. So. (Dang, she make em spicy. I need some water now.) So.

Oh yeah. I see this chat room called *ivory man/ebony woman*, and I had to laugh, first of all, cause I'm wondering why you need a room for that? What in the world could these folks be talking about? But I go in there. I ain't bothered with no white man before, but I ain't adverse. And it don't hurt just to listen to what they got to say. I don't say much at first. I just sit there and keep quiet. My name's there on the screen, blinking R.Mama, for Rasheed's Mama. I read what everybody's saying. A bunch of *my chocolate* this, *my African princess* that and the other thing. And more stuff I didn't even know you could type. Nasty. Real nasty. Rasheed think he slick. "I'm studying, Mama." That's what he's always telling me every time I see him sitting behind that computer.

Now, some dude, his computer name "584LTL," types in "Hello, R.Mama. You're quiet. How are you doing?" I type in "fine" and wait. I don't know nothing about him and I ain't about to start conversating with him like we aces.

"You're a listener," he types. "I like that." I don't say nothing, write nothing, I mean. Plus, I ain't *listening*. I'm *watching*. After a while he types, "R.Mama?" Persistent. So we got to talking, *writing* back and forth. I don't care for talking with somebody but having to write it. When I want to say something, I say it when it's on my mind, you know? But I was having to wait till he typed, then what I typed back came out stiff—and I ain't never been stiff.

He complains about how the men in the room are talking stupid, saying any kind of thing to get a black woman. I'm thinking, well 584TLT, what you in here for, then? But then I'm in the room, too, so I sure can't say nothing. But me and 584TLT end up having decent conversation anyway. Lots of em after that. On the *phone*, honey. We hit it off, me and Andre. That's his real name. But I did ask him. I wanted to know: What did he want with a black woman?

He could count me out of any freaky mess. He kind of laughed when I said that. He said, "You're beautiful, that's all." I couldn't say anything against that, I guess.

One time I did get around to asking him if he made sisters a regularity. It's one thing to satisfy a curiosity (although when I think about that I'm none too cool on it) and an altogether different thing to go through us like tissue paper.

He was on his car phone, driving his Saab down Third Street, he said. Going to dinner. "Let me come get you now. Come on." His voice was silky, even over the car phone. "I'll take you out, we'll really get to know each other."

The "really" part got me. I ain't no fool. I spelled it out for him, clear too, so he could hear me, car phone and all. "I'm not running no pussy drive-through over here. It's going to take a lot more than dinner. Black don't mean 'easy.' We need to get that straight."

He chuckled, which I almost didn't appreciate. I wasn't playing with him. "You mean business, don't you, Norma?"

I didn't say a word. I let that be the answer to his question.

"I mean no disrespect," he said, or at least that's what I think the man said. I mostly heard static. I don't know why folks bother with those damn phones. Anyway, that was the only time before we met that I had to read Andre, make it plain. I kept talking to him, though. Don't ask me where my sense went, cause I couldn't tell you.

Two, three times he kept asking me out. Said he wanted to see me, what I look like. And I ain't in the habit of just going out with all kinds of white men, now. Forget white. Anybody. You liable to see your mama on the news crying, telling folks she ain't seen you for a week, and you stuffed in a trunk somewhere. You know how L.A. is.

But Andre talked like he had some sense. Still wasn't talking about sex—not yet. Didn't sound like he couldn't wait to get his hands around my neck to choke me.

So finally I said all right. Didn't tell Rasheed or La Trice, cause I didn't want to hear it from him, talking to me like he's my daddy. I set this thing up with Andre, fixed it so we'd meet at a place I never never go to. I didn't want to go to my favorite bar and see him sitting up in there every time I went in, in case the meeting went bad, you know. Andre said it was best I set it up, so I'd be comfortable with the situation. Like I even considered going where he wanted, doing what he wanted. I ain't no fool, now. I wait for him at the House of Pies. In the broad daylight. You don't ever catch me in a House of Pies, cause I can't afford the fat. My hips'll spread like water poured on the floor if I eat that stuff. So I don't. I'm already healthy and big-boned as it is.

They know how to make some banana cream pie, though. They don't play. I have me a slice, hurrying up with it because I don't re- ally want to be stuffing my face when this man shows up. While I'm eating, I notice that it's nothing but old folks eating at the counter. Alone. Every one of them. I stopped chewing my pie when I noticed that, thought about how I was sitting at the booth alone, and sud- denly I wanted Andre to hurry up and show up. And he does, so I'm still eating the damn pie when Andre comes through the door. He looks around and then sees me sitting alone. I swear it looked like he was walking up to me in slow motion. I had to put my fork down, OK? The man was fine.

"Norma?" he asks me, and puts out his hand for me to shake it. "Andre."

Now. Andre looked good. Blond hair, sandy really. A little on the wavy side. Bluish eyes. Kind of green, though. Nice lips. *Nice* lips. Full. Had that fresh-scrubbed look about him. But let me tell you something: Andre was a black man, honey. Might not of been *obvious*. Might not of been dark black. Not no *black* black. But black he was, yes sir. Black folks can always tell black folks. I don't care.

So I'm staring at this brother—cause that's what he was, a brother—wondering: does he know this about himself? Will I be ruining his life telling him, "Guess what, man? The party is over." I'm thinking on this when he smiles and says to me, "I thought you'd be blacker." Yes he did, honey. He sure did.

Andre don't know how close he came to banana cream all over his little leather jacket he was sporting. Blacker? How black do you need to be? He had messed up straight away, so I just broke it down to him. "You ain't no white man. Who you think you fooling?" Shoot. I was disappointed. I had it all planned out how I was going to do some educating, some *instructing*. And I wanted to know what he was doing in that chat room in the first place, trying to be "ivory." He looked around, nervous when I hollered he wasn't no white man. Shushed me, too. Yes he did!

Old Andre slid into the booth across from me, all fidgety and twitchy. Telling me to keep it down. I said, "Keep it down! Who you telling to keep it down? Ain't nobody stuttin you and your fake ass!" You talking about a cloud traveling across somebody's face when I cursed him. The *only* dark thing about his face, honey.

"Norma," he said, clasping his big hands together. Nice hands. Gone to waste on some fool. "I'm sorry, but I suppose this isn't going to work, is it?" He ran those hands through his hair and managed a little fake grin.

"Evidently," I said. Salty.

Then he started giving me the eyes, just staring at me. "Where you from?"

"Louisiana," I said. Like it was any of his goddamn business, excuse my French.

"Oh," he says. "That explains it. Creoles and all that."

Ooooo no he *didn't.*

"What is wrong with you?" I asked him. I was waving my hand for my check and just dying to get up out of there. I sho made the right choice about the House of Pies, cause Andre had done messed up the place for me. Wasn't no need of me worried about coming back around there for some pie, else I be liable to run into crazy Andre. Keep some fat off my hips for sure.

"Nothing is wrong with me, Norma." Had the nerve to try and get snotty on me, too. "You are the one looking for white men. I'm a black man looking for a black woman."

But he left the part out about him trying to be white! Trying to call *me* out! Made me mad cause he was talking to me like he *knew* me. And that's the part that made me mad. People always think they got the 411 on you when they done only met you five minutes before. I had had me enough of Andre, told him so, and he got up and left, but not before he gave me one more snotty look and more attitude.

"Norma," he says, "normally, because I'm a gentleman, I say that it has been a pleasure. But it hasn't been. Good afternoon."

And then after I invited Andre to kiss my behind, he left.

I'm not going on and on about no dumb-ass Andre, but the man told me he ain't going around telling people he's white. He just don't correct them if they think it! OK? No lie. And more junk about how hard it is to find a good black woman, is what he told me. A black man, passing for white, looking for a black, *black* woman to hang on his arm. And me disappointed (just for a second, now, don't get me wrong) that the man wasn't white for real. Unh, unh, unh.

It used to be that folks was just folks, you know? Now, seems like folks are *weird* folks all the way round. They can't make it easy for you to be with them, they have to come at you with all kinds of craziness, like goofy-ass Andre and the rest, a list that just goes on and on, honey.

That's what I try to tell my daughter who thinks she's going to catch a rich man on her looks alone: catching a man that's just rich ain't gone cut it. You be looking for somebody that fit just one thing, and you get a world of stuff with that package—not just that one thing. Old Andre was a package and a half!

So that's what I just came from. And I most certainly need a taste. You can talk about a woman in a bar having a drink all by herself— easy, desperate, whatever you want to call her. But sometimes the days turn out just like my man two stools down with that loose tie hanging around his neck. The world is crazy. And Rasheed can have all that online mess. Nothing but weird. Andre probably had his trunk all lined up with pillows and blankets and a hatchet waiting for my silly ass.

Least I come in here and see who and what I'm talking to right off the bat. Ain't no screens and rooms with freaky names. I see a man, right away I see if he's fine or not. I talk to him proper, over a drink like you supposed to. Hey, Rickie! One more for the road, honey—or two. I'm gone let the drinks flow and see what he's got to offer.

Not like I'm looking for something. Cause I ain't.

something to remember me by

You will celebrate with us, my dying cousin West called up to inform me. You will come out, get out of that lint box you call an apartment, get up off your behind. Do something.

"Why are you guys celebrating?" I asked.

"You need a reason?" West said. "Oh, and you can't call folks no more? You lost my number? Aunt Norma say you act like you can't be bothered with nobody. What's wrong with you?" He hung up the phone before I could answer. My mother was always telling everyone, including me, how I acted and how I felt. Now, as I lie sprawled out on the floor of my new apartment, watching them drink liquor that I suddenly had to provide from Mac's Liquor across the street, West's boyfriend wants to know: "What happened to your leg, Cuz?" He's calling me that now, just like West, like he's my cousin, like we go way back instead of just meeting each other last month.

"Lord, don't get her started on how I *threw* her off the porch. Every time she tell it, it gets wilder and crazier." West picks up his jelly jar of tequila, the one with Dino and Pebbles, and then jangles the ice. "Nice glasses. If you're trying to get housewarming gifts, it's working." He throws back his head to finish the drink and chews loudly on a mouthful of ice. The crunch of it sounds like gravel grounding underneath a tire on a dirt road, which ties into the story of how I got the scar that runs from my knee down my shin, all the way down to my ankle. I love to tell this story.

"Now. This is the thing—"

"Wait." West pours more tequila into his and Marshall's glasses, and then into my glass shaped like a Buddha with a handle on it, a souvenir from the Japanese restaurant Beni Hana. Then he gives me a squeeze of lemon. "Not that you need any more help, with your lying self." He sits back on my dingy blue futon, one of three pieces of furniture in my studio, and Marshall gently rubs the back of West's bald head. They both look at me like a show's about to begin. West adores this story. There's sweat on his head, like little drops of oil on a large mound of dark chocolate, and I can see the beginnings of the crescent-shaped scar that starts from one ear, travels around the base of his skull, and ends at the other ear. Now, I don't particularly care to tell the story.

I lean back on both arms and stretch my legs out in front of me. The scar on my right shin is dark and fibrous like tree roots. I cover the scar with my other leg. "We should get going if you intend to match me drink for drink tonight. Before the two of you get too drunk."

"Too drunk?" West frowns. "Ain't no such thang."

Marshall tilts his head in agreement and clinks his glass with West's. "The leg, April. First tell me the story. Then we go." He leans forward and strokes his sandy goatee. His gray eyes are laughing.

I stand up and take their glasses, which aren't empty, and Marshall picks a piece of lint from my brown corduroy skirt before I take the three steps required to get me to the kitchen sink. "West'll tell you. I just fell off a porch one summer when we were visiting our grandmother down South."

"Right. Stop trying to perpetrate and give my man the real deal." West wipes his head with a handkerchief he keeps in his back pocket. He folds it neatly and then stands to put it back in his pocket. He looks strong, big and boxy—scary, with all his hair shaved. Somebody you ought not mess with. But all the sweating, that's a change in him, and I don't like it. My one-room apartment feels too small for him, for Marshall, and me. When he sits back down he says, "She did fall off a porch. But she fell when she could of jumped. And she didn't jump cause she's scary. We were trying to see who could make the biggest jump, but she got scared cause the porch was too high, so she said."

I squirt some dishwashing liquid onto a greasy, crumbly sponge that should be thrown out and begin to wash the glasses, but I turn and raise an eyebrow to this. "It *was* too high. And you didn't have to throw me, either."

"Push. Just a little push is what it was."

"Well, whatever you want to call it, my leg's a mess, thanks to you," I say, glancing down at it. But sometimes I actually don't mind the scar. "I look like I did a tour of duty."

I laugh aloud when I remember why we were jumping in the first place, not merely to see who could jump the farthest, but whether all of us could hit the mark and then get taken to Loretta Lynn's Dude Ranch. Our mean cousin, Larry, who by the end of that summer had tried to disguise hair removal lotion in a shampoo bottle and then given it to me to wash my hair, said that if West and I hit the mark, he'd get his mother to take us all.

"What are you laughing at?" West asks, his voice gurgling from the ice he's chewing on.

"You were so mad at me for blowing our Loretta Lynn trip. Jesus. Loretta Lynn."

"Loretta was the shit. Don't play like you was too cool for Loretta. I was pissed because you wouldn't even *try*. You wanted *proof* we were going before you even tried to jump. Shoot, I jumped and asked about the details later. And I had to throw your scary ass because you was messing with our chances! Whining about the porch being too high."

Marshall thoughtfully strokes his goatee some more, like psychoanalysts on old TV shows. "That doesn't sound like you, West. Pushing her off the porch like that." His face is glowing pink from their weekend in Palm Springs. I'm thinking that Marshall has no idea what sounds like West when he's only known him two months, the two of them acting as though they've been together for years. Made for each other. "You can't just go falling in love with folks," I told West the first time I met Marshall—and liked him.

"*You* can't," he said. "But I can."

I let the glasses drip on a dish drainer. After wiping my hands dry on my skirt, I lean with my back against the sink and hug myself, watching the two of them. West gazes absently out of the window at the swarthy Marlboro man who scowls into the apartment from a billboard across the street, and Marshall tugs at the black decorative yarn that sprouts from the futon. From the open window, I can hear cars slowly merging onto the Hollywood freeway below, the dull thump of bass music from the stereos mixed with chugging engines.

West says, "The throwing-off part isn't so unusual about me, really, but April trying to act like she can fight somebody, that's the funny part. She got up from that road with rocks and dirt and blood stuck on her shins and came on swinging. Muhammad Ali." He grins at me. "For once. That's what I like about that scar. For once. Usually, she was busy trying to look cute."

I stick my tongue out at West.

"You hit West? You guys actually fought?" Marshall's concerned, holds up his fists and punches into the air.

"We were just kids, so it wasn't a real fight. Not really." When West stands and stretches, I hear his knees crack. "But I still gave her something to remember me by."

Marshall is silent, and so am I, because I hate the sound of what West has said.

"Are we going dancing, or what? Because I feel like dancing," I say, walking to the window and peering down on the freeway. I prefer to dance, rather than reminisce. The screen in the window between myself and the outside is black with dirt. I wipe off the smudge I suspect is left on my forehead from pressing against the screen.

"We're dancing," West says.

"But first, we grub," Marshall demands. "I want a big ol' fat and greasy Tommy Burger with extra chili."

"That stuff is toxic. It'll kill you," I say, immediately sorry I said it. West will start, crack what he thinks is a joke, always talking about death and dying in flip sarcastic ways to get me to laugh, as if laughing will make me forget he's dying.

Marshall stands behind West and hugs him. "Did you guys ever get to go to Loretta's Lynn's ranch? Was it cool and all? Did you ride horses?"

"Please," I say. "Larry was a liar, like always, and come to find out, Loretta Lynn's had Civil War reenactments and stuff. What's that all about?"

West twirls his car keys around his finger. "So? It could have been fun, you never know. And for once, Larry could have been telling the truth. I'm a gambling man." He turns to face Marshall. "You ready?" he says to me. "Cause I'm ready," he says without waiting for an answer. Then—and I knew this was coming—"I don't think I need to worry about death by chili burger," he says flatly. It's not funny, what he says. Just true.

West drives a red Karmann Ghia, a sports car much too small for him, much too small for all of us to ride in, but he insists on his car, not mine. The night is clear, he says. The air is clean. The night is young. The San Gabriel Mountains we can touch, if we try. "On a night like this," he asks, "you'd rather ride around in a funky old Buick that looks like something Uncle Toots drives? Please."

Marshall says he feels guilty that I'm the one who has to fold myself into the back of the car because I'm shorter. He offered to sit in the back, but he's six foot two, which is ridiculous. *OK, I see why West loves you*, I thought, watching him realize how impossible it would be for him to sit there moments after he insisted. He's twisted around in his seat, yelling conversation to me. But the wind catches nearly everything.

"—Rage!" I catch the last word before he turns back around to direct West's driving. He means the club Rage, where we'll go tonight. Earlier, when Marshall said it was a good mixed bar, that I'd feel more comfortable, I thought he meant racially mixed. West rolled his eyes and said that sometimes, if he didn't know I was born and raised in L.A., he could swear I was straight-up country. I said there wasn't nothing wrong with being country, something my mother would say, who's as Tennessee as they come.

We've already had three near misses, minutes away from Tommy's. West drives his car as though there simply are no road rules, speeding only to slam on the brakes inches from the car ahead, suddenly swerving into the next lane to avoid having to stop because the car ahead of him has slowed down. I think, *Just because you're dying doesn't mean you have to drive like the rest of us can go, too.* Then I think: *I'm sorry, God. I take it back.*

I get scared that bad things will happen to me when I think that way. "God don't like ugly," my mother always says, and I could get cancer, too, just like that. But these days, even this is something I could say to West, right to his face. He'd laugh.

Like he laughs at my pinch to his neck as he races into a parking spot at the burger stand, making people clutch their food, whatever it is covered with chili, and step up the pace to get out of his way. This place reminds me of a long time ago when the waitresses took your order and carried your food on roller skates. Except here, after the cook yells at you, "What are you having!" you get in a car and eat your food or you stand and eat at a counter that makes a U around the inside of the parking lot. Marshall has made it clear that car dining isn't an option, thank God, and right there is reason number two for West loving him: he knows when to be polite and he knows when to be sensible. When the cook barks the question to Marshall, he orders a chili burger, chili fries, and a tamale smothered in chili, plus two cans of iced tea. Then he turns to me and West. "What do you guys want?"

I order a burger with so much chili, extra chili, that everything will get all over me, if I'm not careful. If I'm not careful, I'll be a mess, ketchup dribbled down the front of my shirt, onions and chili dropped down my spandex top. After we've made our way to the wooden counters painted lime-green, I snatch a series of paper towels from their silver holder and cover myself with them like a child wearing a bib.

"You cannot be for real," West says, lowering his already half-eaten burger and giving me his quizzical are-you-high look.

"This food's rather messy. If I eat without a napkin it'll be too messy and I'll have to go back home and change or something."

"And then your life will be over," he says. He drops his burger into the cardboard box and wipes his hands and mouth much too roughly with his paper towel. Then he balls it up and tosses it in with his left-over food.

"Did I miss the part where someone explained why this is a big deal?" I ask, snotty like he hates.

Marshall, in the middle, looks to West and then looks to me. Finally, he says, "Are you going to eat that?" and takes West's burger and puts it with the rest of his stash. He probably truly wants to change the subject, prevent a fight. This much, at least, Marshall knows about West—and about me at this point. West and I had argued when I first met Marshall, his therapist of sorts, whose job it is to help West make the transition from living to dying. "We like to say, 'From dying to living,'" Marshall corrected me. Why anyone would set out to make such a job their life, I cannot figure.

"Isn't this a conflict of interest?" I lowered my voice as the waiter placed my lasagna in front of me. "And isn't this a little too soon? To be engaged in this sort of relationship?"

"The too-soon part," West said, cutting his spaghetti into small bits, hacking it, really. "Well, I'm not even going to take the conversation to that level. And the conflict of interest part, ain't nobody conflicted but you. Pass me the bread."

I looked at Marshall, who was studying his eggplant. When he got no answer there, he looked up and smiled at me faintly. Then he started with the stroking of the goatee.

West was just getting warmed up. "You know so much, where's Mel?"

West knew where Mel was. Two months before, Mel had proposed to me, and I made a disaster of if. We had sat in front of the TV eating ramen and watching the local news.

"We're so boring," Mel had said, placing his bowl of noodles on the coffee table. He gathered his long black hair prematurely streaked with gray, twisted it, and then wrapped it around into a tight bun. He often wore his hair like that, grocery shopping and doing other errands. His smooth brown face, the striking cheekbones that were so prominent with his hair pulled back, was what most people paid attention to, not the fact that he was a man wearing his hair in a bun. "I mean, don't you think?" He crossed his arms and looked at me. He was amused, but I didn't know why.

"What?" I shrugged.

"It's Friday night, we're watching this depressing crap." He gestured toward the picture before us. "We should be out—somewhere—and you should be in a tight black dress, some guy looking down your cleavage, and me stepping up to him to say, 'Sorry, loser, this one's mine.'"

I dropped my fork in the plastic microwaveable soup bowl. "That sounds boring, except for the 'some guy' part." I grinned and then touched his hand. "I like this. You know that?"

"I do know that," he said. "And that's why I want to ask you something. Did you hear that?" He pointed to the side door leading to the back yard. My eyes followed his finger.

"I didn't hear anything," I said. When I turned back to my ramen, there was a tiny diamond ring sitting on top of the noodles.

"Mel," I said tiredly, "what are you doing?"

"What's it look like?"

"I told you—"

"I know what you told me, but I'm asking you again." He picked up the remote and turned off the TV. The newscaster was interrupted mid-sentence. "You're not ready, et cetera. But you're the *one*. Aren't you tired of shacking up?" He took my bowl from me and placed it next to his on the table. The ring still sat there in the soup. He grabbed my wrists. "If you love me, care anything about me, it should be so easy to say 'yes.' I want you to put this ring on, say 'yes.'"

I looked down at his big hands enclosing my wrists. "I need more time."

"Time for what?" Mel drew a deep breath and then exhaled. He let my hands go.

I kept my eyes on his left hand, which had raised, cream-colored scars on the knuckles from when he accidently slammed his hand in the car door. But I couldn't articulate what I needed time for.

Mel waited a moment for me to speak up. When I didn't, he said, "Look." He took his hair down and scratched his scalp. "We can do this. You don't even want to try? You—*we*—could do this marriage thing. Look at me." He held my face in his hands, kissed me on the tip of my nose. When he pulled back, he stared at me with vast, unwavering eyes the color of whiskey. "Be my wife."

What if we ended up hating each other, divvying up the kids for the holidays and summer vacations? What if I ended up hating the way he chewed his food, the way his toes pointed inward when he walked? What if I could do better? The do-better part, I didn't mention to Mel.

"What are you talking about? We don't even have kids yet. Do we?" Mel lifted one of the pillows on the couch we got at the Goodwill for ten dollars and felt under it. "What if, what if, what if. I tell you what: you wear that phrase out, don't you?" He sighed and reached over to pick the ring out of the bowl, cleaning it with his T-shirt. "I'm holding onto this for two months. Two months, April. Then I go. I can't stay with a woman who doesn't want to be with me." His voice broke on the last word, but I pretended not to hear it.

Mel was sure I'd say yes, but by the second month, when he realized I wasn't going to go, he got angry instead of hurt, threatened to take everything in the house with him, which wasn't much. It wasn't like him. When he left, he did take everything, as though I'd marry him just because I needed a chair or a wine glass. I wanted to tell him not to leave this way, that I just needed more time. But I didn't. I let him go.

West said he would have followed a man as fine as Mel to a Ku Klux Klan rally and damn well enjoy himself, too. He said I'd gone from bad to worse, waiting for a rich man to come along and sweep me off my feet. I had watched West polish off his wine and take a forkful of my lasagna. "Don't be an asshole, and don't talk to me about Mel," I said to him. And then I asked Marshall, "So. How do you like your job?"

"I swear to God I'm not getting on any freeway," I say to West as we pull out of Tommy's. "It's dangerous. I've got no seat belt back here." I fully expected him to take the freeway, driving eighty in the fast lane, only to say, "See? I told you you'd be OK," when we got to our destination. But tonight he takes the streets, "to be in the middle of where it's at."

We ride in silence, West playing gospel music on his stereo, the wind blowing hot against our faces. The songs are gospel on the funky side, so that you forget they're singing about meeting your Maker, walking right as rain, the highway to heaven. They've turned it into dance music, and West's bobbing his head and snapping his fingers. Marshall turns the sound up when one of his favorites begins.

My first time in church that I can remember, the first time I heard live gospel music, I was visiting relatives in Tennessee. The reverend hollered and pointed and stomped his feet, stopping only to wipe his dripping brow. And when the choir sang, the ladies in the front row screamed, and the organ was so thick and loud I couldn't breathe. I ran down the aisle and out of the church. Auntie Mavis came after me and asked me what was the matter. I was only seven years old. "I feel funny," I said. I held my stomach and bent over as if I were going to throw up. But that wasn't the feeling I had. I felt as though I was going to cry. I felt like laughing, as though I was going to shout. "Auntie Mavis, it feels like I ain't got no clothes on."

She peered at me. "Ain't got no what?"

"Clothes on."

"Well, ain't that something to say." She knelt down and held my face in her hands, then she put her hand on my forehead.

"No fever," she said. "You look fine. Might be you just getting the spirit." She winked. She retied the blue ribbon woven through one of my pigtails and took my hand to walk back into the church. I sat under her for the rest of the service, scared and squeezing my eyes shut, trying to keep out the spirit.

I grab onto Marshall's seat and lean forward. "Hey. What else you got up there to play?"

West throws his head back. "Like what?" he says, shouting to the sky.

"Whatever. Anything else."

He rifles through his glove compartment, peers into it a little too long before putting his eyes back on the road. But he doesn't pick up any tapes to see what they are.

"Sorry!" he shouts. "Fresh out of 'whatever.'"

We stop at a red light. "Look," West says. He points to a pink stucco house on the corner before us. In the living room, four little kids are in step doing a dance routine. Their backs are turned to the blue light of the TV.

"What are they watching?" Marshall asks, craning his neck. "I'm always interested."

Three of the kids are girls with long curly hair, and then there's a boy on the end. "That must be their brother," I say, leaning in between West and Marshall.

"'Member, Cuz? We used to do that, make up all kinds of crazy dances. Until you lost any kind of rhythm you had." That, I laugh at, because it's true. West shifts gears when the light changes, jerking me back into my yoga-like position in the back seat.

West and I are always interested in what's going on in other people's houses. When I see light shining from the windows, I wonder what their lives are like. What are they thinking, who do they know, what do they know? Or when I see other people driving their cars, speeding past me on the freeway, maybe someone's reclined on the passenger side, their bare foot sticking out the window, jiggling to music blaring from the stereo. I want to be with them. Every place

I'm not always seems a better place to be. I think, *Take me with you.*
You are not arguing with your cousin about why he's already talking about what clothes he will wear at his funeral, asking him, "Why
do you always have to talk about it?" Begging him, "I don't want to
talk about it." He is not telling you that, white three-piece suit or not,
he will be dead. And he will have to wear something.

"Just like you will be alive," he has said. "And you will have to get
on with it."

Rage opens into the street. The front of the bar has no walls, so the
crowd can drink and look out onto the sidewalk, which Marshall and
West do not want to do.

"Oh no. We came here to dance. Ain't no standing around!"
Marshall yells over repetitive, urgent disco. He's already sounding
like West.

"And drink, though, too!" West adds, and spins around, clowning.

Marshall pulls his wallet from his back pocket and leans into my
ear. "What can I get you, April?"

I shake my head. "I'm fine."

He points at West, eyebrow raised, waiting. The black light of the
bar makes Marshall's shorts blinding white.

Over the music, West screams, "Tequila!" and Marshall dances to
the bar.

We're on the edge of the dance floor, and West can't stand still.
He's marching to the music, surveying the crowd. Finally, he grabs
me, pulls my right arm out with his left. "Tango with me!" he
hollers, and I stumble with him briefly before he gives up. I can't
seem to grab onto Marshall and West's festive mood. He studies me
and then puts his lips to my ear, cups his hand around his mouth.
"I'm sorry I got an attitude about the paper towel earlier. If you want

to look crazy, that's your business." He stands back and grins. He's already sweating. I shake my head and punch him in the shoulder. He knows that means don't worry about it.

Marshall has two tiny glasses of tequila. "Fourteen dollars! Bastards!" He holds the glasses out to us so we can share the outrage, then he gives West his drink and pulls him onto the dance floor.

West reaches for me, but misses. "You're the one who wanted to come out," he tells me. Before he can try again, Marshall pulls him away. They're swallowed up by the crowd just like that.

If I can just take my time, watch everybody else, I can get into this. Start to have a good time. I lean against the sticky bar and order ginger ale. While I'm watching, waiting for my drink, I feel a tap on my shoulder and turn to a copper-brown, baby face with large, dark, intelligent eyes and a toothy grin.

"Would you like to dance?" He extends his hand. Yes, she would, West would say, if he were here. But he's not. When I hesitate, the man drops his hand. "I'm not trying to cruise you or anything. I'm here alone, and I just want to have a good time. You know." I stare at him long enough for him to finally offer, "I'm gay. Like everybody here?" He runs a hand through curly hair that's soaked. "So you know. I'm harmless." He grins at me.

His linen shirt is sticking to his muscular chest. He blinks long eyelashes. My eyes won't leave his.

"I'm waiting," I say. "For my husband. He went to the bathroom."

"I'm sorry," he says, embarrassed by my poorly executed lie. He holds his arms high like he's being held up and backs away.

The man's rich skin reminds me of Mel's. I mostly remember his back, my last week with him. He had stood barefoot in the kitchen, methodically wrapping glasses in last week's newspapers and carelessly tossing the glasses into a box. He heard me come in, I could tell by the sudden straightness of his backbone, a few beads of water from his shower still glistening in the shallow groove down the center of his smooth back. His hair, still damp, hung in thick, shiny strings well past his shoulders. It was time for his trim, which I always did.

"If you want," I said, "I could give you a trim. If you want."

He didn't answer me, but put down a half-wrapped glass. I went to him, put my arms around him and rubbed my cheeks against his buttery skin.

"I want you to touch me," Mel said after a while. "That's what I want."

Mel had been sleeping on the couch in the living room for three days, ignoring me when I asked him to come to bed and leaving me alone on the couch when I came to him. This anger from him was something I'd never seen before. I wanted to tell him, "See, this is the sort of thing that could have happened to us if we got married." But still, I believed that if I could get him inside of me he would change his mind. He wouldn't leave me. And so, when he asked me to touch him, I thought that I had him back. I found the top button of his jeans and unfastened it, and then the next button. Mel stood very still, his heart pounding so hard that I could almost feel it touching me through his back. I slid my right hand inside the front of his jeans, and I felt his belly flutter. But then he pulled my hand out and held both of my hands tightly. His hands were cool and dry from handling the newspaper.

"No," he said. "This is too easy for you."

"What?" When he turned to face me, I was smiling. "I *like* easy," I said, flirting.

"I know," he said, and buttoned his jeans. "April," he said, in a voice that was sad and far away. And then he picked up the half-wrapped glass and finished wrapping it.

The drink that's placed in front of me at the bar is not what I ordered. It's something strong and bitter, with a lime swimming in it. I pay the bartender anyway, because I don't want to fight about it, and leave the drink—mostly ice—sitting there to turn watery and weak. And I watch people. I watch them throw their heads back, mouths wide open, laughing. I watch them show off silly dance steps to amuse their partners. I watch them leaning into each other, straining to talk as one hand holds a drink and the other hand slices and strokes the air for emphasis. I look for West. I keep looking but can't find him, and panic strikes me just as suddenly as it disappears, as though I've almost fallen but regained my footing.

West appears, like a magic trick, and gently slips his arm around my waist. He smells of sweat and baby powder. "I was going to the bar to get robbed, but why don't you dance with us?"

I cup my hand over my mouth. "Where's Marshall?"

"Out there." He flips his hand vaguely toward the dance floor. "Trying to act like he can dance. I want to dance with you." West grabs my wrist and pulls me after him, but I yank away. "Girl, I ain't playing with you," he says, grinning. "Now come on!" He holds me tightly. The more I try to break free, the stronger his grip becomes. He's starting to drag me closer to the dance floor, between clusters of smiling people. I want to slap him. He's happy, easily so. I'm not, and I've got a long life to live, as far as I know.

I let my hand go limp, as if I've given up. When he loosens his grip, I push him. I'm thinking as I push him that I mean it all as a joke. I push him much too hard for it to be funny, and he grabs onto me before we both stumble into a startled man whose drink falls onto the floor, shattering into glitzy bits. West ends up on his knees. Stunned, he stares at me openmouthed. Several pairs of hands grab at us to help us to our feet. I've got a cut on my hand.

"What is wrong with you!" West's eyes flash and then study me thoughtfully when he sees that my eyes are watery. He nods a thank-you to the people who helped us up and they all blend back into the pumping mass. He swipes his knees as he approaches me, looks at his hands before rubbing them on his jeans.

"I'm sorry, West." I barely raise my voice to overcome the music, so I'm not sure that he's heard me. He holds a hand out to me, which I take, and guides me to a more quiet end of the bar where two men are kissing. We prop ourselves against the hard, cracked vinyl lining of the bar.

I hold my bloody palm up to show him. "More souvenirs of you."

West wipes my palm with a cocktail napkin at the bar and starts applying pressure, even though the cut isn't that bad. "Yep. I have to keep trying until you get it right."

"I want to go home," I say finally.

West wipes his head with his soaked handkerchief, drags it down and around his neck, pats his forehead, chin, and cheeks as if he's blessing himself. I wait for him to get in my face about pushing him. Instead, he says, "This is a celebration, remember?" He speaks as though he's reminding me that this is merely a going-away party.

I want him to understand that he is leaving me behind. He is leaving us all behind. "You're dying, remember? So, forgive me. I'm fresh out of confetti."

"Dying, honey, not dead." West takes my cut hand and squeezes it hard. So hard, I wince. And then he leaves me.

I resist saying, "Wait," because even if he did, I wouldn't know where to go from here. So I wait instead, watch and wait for West to come back.

Next to me at the bar a tall, unsteady man pulls wadded bills out of his pocket to order a drink. He hunches over, unwrinkling the money, smoothing it out. Counting and recounting it, as if he can't believe that's all he has left.

At least, if I wasn't going to dance, I could have brought my camera. Pictures of this, of West having the time of his life, I'm going to want someday. I spot West dancing alone, then with a group of people, then with Marshall. West is dancing hard, I can see the sweat glistening on his body. But he's tired. I know. His moves are sloppy, and he's struggling to keep up with the beat. The strobe light suspends his actions just for a moment, freezing him in time and then releasing him, making his movement jerky, just like the haunted house skeletons that we used to see at the Long Beach Pike when we were kids. Before they tore it down. Marshall sees me watching and waves his arms wildly like he's flagging down a car for help. His mouth forms exaggeratedly enunciated words. *Come on*, he says, motioning for me, calling me.

But I can't. I can't take a step.

markers

When my big brother calls me up and tells me to do something, I do it. That's all. He couldn't drive mama to do her errand today because of his double-shift at the sprinkler factory, but somebody ought to, because it's one of the hottest days on California record, and our Mama ain't got no business standing around waiting for a bus on a day like this, and could I drive out and do it? he asked. Told.

Driving with my mother, I'm imagining all the things I will have to do when I get back home to Max, who will be there waiting to loudly tick off all the items I will have inevitably forgotten. All the tomatoes I've chosen that are too firm or too soft, asking me why did I buy the cheeses at the cheap local market, *disgusting,* when I should have gone to the gourmet market where, any idiot knows, they have the best cheeses, Avery, he'll say. And then he will start on how late I am, where have I *been?* What have I been *doing* all this time? All that time just to run an errand with my mother? But because he and my mother don't know each other so well, not even after four years, he will have no idea how these things can take so much time, how maddening it can be that my mother doesn't know where she is going.

She never knows, because in all her fifty-six years she's never learned how to drive. She relies on markers, like they used to when she lived in Arkansas, I guess. *When you see the tree stump down the road, turn right.* That kind of stuff. My visits with her turn into taking her here or there, around and around, looking for a place, only to end up where we left off, nowhere near where we need to be.

It's 102 degrees and my Jaguar has no air-conditioning. The car's old — 1975 — and hasn't got much else going for it, really, except several dents in the body and expensive engine problems. This car was one of those Max ideas that seemed like a good one at the time. He was tired of getting phone calls from me, broken down, whining to be saved from odd places at odd times. I couldn't afford a new car, so he bought me this one. One thing I could afford was to paint over the dull, peeling brown, so I did. Red. Because if I'm going to have a classy car, I want it to look good, at least.

"You need to keep it clean. That's what you need to do," my mother always says. "You got all kinds of Wendy's and Burger King papers and whatnot, talking about painting it. You throwing bad money after bad!" she said after I told her about my paint job.

She doesn't get it, my mother. She thinks sparkling clean-on-the-inside makes the same statement as clean on the outside, the kind of thinking that's the most frustrating thing about her. She thinks either/or, and is always saying *why don't you just.*

"Why don't you just make a right here?" she says.

We've done that, turned right, turned here so many times that there's no number for it. Still, I turn right. We're driving the San Gabriel Valley, somewhere in parched Pomona. I'm anxious. I'm not comfortable in these broken-down neighborhoods. They bother me, like not being able to rest until you figure out a forgotten name, reminding me of when I was a little girl and lived in South Central L.A.

It's painfully hot in my car. The heat and the smog are too much. Something bad and unhealthy must be happening to me and to my mother. Because what is it in the air that makes our eyes water and burn so much? And yet, my mother doesn't say anything about the heat. I actually whimper, but she wipes her brow with a wrinkled tissue in silence.

The heat waves above the pavement make everything seem like I'm looking at it through an orange, smoggy film. For reasons that I haven't been able to afford to find out all summer, and because I won't overcome my stubbornness to ask Max for money to help me fix it, heat blows out of my car's vents, though the heater is off. As we pass the same Boys Market for the third time, I feel the irritating tickle of a bead of sweat traveling between my breasts.

I yell at my mother. "How could you not know where this place is, Mom? How many times have you been here? You always do this." I flip down my sun visor because it gives me something to do, like counting to ten before you say or do something you'll be sorry for later. I drive hunched over the steering wheel, gripping it, as if somehow the intensity of these actions will help us find the food stamp office. I hear my words long after I've said them. Ten years ago, when I felt like I was the kid and she was the parent, my mother would have popped me. But at twenty-eight, I'm too old for that.

"The bus route is different from the way we came. I don't usually get a ride here," she says, and I look at her, expecting a face of accusation and instead her face is full of gratitude. "There," my mother says, pointing to a mini-mall on our right that looks like twelve others we've passed in an hour.

"We've *been* here," I say, "passed it about five times."

"Well," my mother says, getting her paperwork together, "sorry, Love, but this is it."

As I pull into the parking lot I'm almost sorry that we've found the place, though ten minutes ago all I wanted out of life was to be here. The mini-mall lot is crammed with people trying to get food stamps, checks cashed, bus passes, and junk from the ninety-nine-cent store. I can't take hot *and* people, not this kind of hot, not so many people, and all I can think of is how, on top of everything, this is going to make me even later than I already am to help Max with his dinner party.

"This is awful," I say. We crawl slowly through the lot in search of a spot. "How long do you think this is going to take?" Before my mother can answer, I cut her off.

"Bitch," I say, and give the finger to a young woman in a rusted-out Oldsmobile who has taken my parking space. When I was living in my parents' house, I could never swear, and I feel funny but don't apologize for it, because that doesn't seem right, either, as though I've passed that point of little-girl concessions. I end up parking next to the woman who has taken my spot, and when I get out I glare at her. She looks at me coolly and glassy-eyed. She takes her time walking to me, like she's bored with the fact that she's got to be bothered. She's inches from my face.

"Watch. Who. You. Mess. With." She states each word deliberately, each one digging a deep hole for me to get thrown into with the dirt packed tight. She's Tootsie Roll-colored, with dark brown irises surrounded by blue-white hair pulled back tightly in a bun, and except for her stubby height, looks just like me. But I'm afraid of her.

I glance at my mother, who has gotten out of the car but says nothing. She looks at me with raised eyebrows. I know that she won't say anything to help me. It's not her way.

In the lifetime of two seconds it takes me to decide what to do, I back down.

"Let's go, Mom." I turn my back on the woman, and my mother and I find our way to the line moving post-office slow. The loudness of this hole-in-the-wall is unbearable—little kids running all over the place screaming and crawling across the floor, parents screaming at their kids just as loudly.

"Look at these little bad-ass kids." My mother shakes her head. "I would have wore you out, running around acting crazy."

I cough out a quick laugh and my mother laughs with me. I realize it's been a long time since we've laughed together. It embarrasses me.

"Nicky!" a young woman calls out. "I'ma beat your ass if you don't get over here right now! I told you to stick close to me!"

"Look here." My mother taps my shoulder. "I need to go to that ninty-nine-cent store after we done here."

I stand on my toes a bit out of line to see how many people are ahead of us. Two, which could very well take two hours. "Why do you need to go there?" I ask, and before my mother can answer I say, "I may not have time because I'm having some people over tonight. Besides, the stuff in there is cheap, it's junk, Mom."

"Same reason I need to come here."

"What?" I've forgotten I even asked her a question and I'm distracted because as we approach the bullet-proof glass of the clerk I see it's the Oldsmobile woman. She looks through me.

"How you doing today?" my mother asks her, slipping her plastic food stamp card and identification under the window. The woman ignores my mother. "Hot today, ain't it?" my mother tries again. I want to say, *Mom, don't waste your time*, and that's another thing about her: being nice to people who treat her like crap. I want to pull her aside and tell her this in hushed tones, like mothers do to their kids when they're setting them straight.

"I like your nails," my mother says to the clerk. The nails are hideous orange fake claws, probably done at the nail salon three doors down.

"Where's your other green ID card?" the woman states flatly, as though she hasn't heard a word my mother has said.

My mother's mouth forms an **O** and her eyes widen. "Don't you know I left it at home. I can't believe I did that."

I take off my sunglasses to see better. I can't believe what I'm hearing. I've driven from Santa Monica, one hour, for nothing.

"Can you take information from my other card, anyway? It's kind of hard for me to get here," my mother says politely. It's agonizing, like she's begging. The woman shoves my mother's cards back at us. I'm realizing that if my mother can't get her food stamps now, we'll have to drive the half hour back to her house in West Covina and come back. I don't want to come back here.

"You'll have to come back," the clerk says as if programmed.

"But—"

"You'll have to come back. That's all to it. Next."

I panic. "My mother needs these stamps today. We can't come back."

The clerk leans towards the dull, silver-colored speaker hanging in the middle of the glass partition. "Miss Fancy Car," she says, real low. I can barely hear her. "I think you can wait another day for your food stamps, OK? Now collect your shit and move on before I go off on your ass." Her eyes are on my mother when she says this, and my mother looks shaken. I want her to fight the clerk, to let her know who she's talking to. But I know she won't.

I grab my mother's cards from underneath the glass and before I turn to leave I say, "My car and I have nothing to do with my mother."

I hurry to my car, leaving my mother behind. I can barely get my key in the door because I'm so impatient to get out of here and take my mother home so I can go home. I remember she wants to go to the store. "You still want to go to the store?" I ask, but the way I ask it, it sounds like *You better not want to go to the damn store.* My mother shakes her head.

"No. Take me home."

She's quiet on the way back to her house. A bad habit I learned from my father, who could hardly find the words to talk at any given time and place, who found it especially painful in the closed-in space of a car, is to turn on the radio immediately—turn it up and only turn it down if somebody is saying something to me, or me to them. I particularly don't like to talk much when I'm driving the freeway because I can't do both at the same time.

So the radio's playing an oldie by the Platters. "Only You." But my mother's quiet makes me uneasy, so I talk.

I ask her about her job search, which isn't going well. She thinks that she can't find work because of bad luck or because she isn't looking hard enough. She thinks simply working hard will get her somewhere, like when she was a girl and could just sew people's clothes to make a living. She's old-fashioned. I don't tell her what I know: that she's a fifty-six-year-old woman with an eighth-grade education, that all the hard work in the world won't change the fact that that's not enough anymore. This is difficult to know. So instead I say something easy, something that I halfway believe—"Mom, everything will turn out OK"—and drive on down the Pomona freeway.

When we first moved to the suburbs, my father of course had a job. He was a factory worker in L.A. commuting back and forth. But my mother had to work two jobs so that we could afford the house. Our new house had a lawn. There were no gunshots at night. We didn't even lock the doors. That summer before school started, before I started looking at myself with different eyes, these things were good enough.

In the motel rooms cleaned by my mother, I would stay out of her way and do homework in a corner. But I would sometimes leave slips of paper with her initials written on them, like a signature. Sometimes I left them under the beds or in between the folds of a towel hardened by the water and chemicals it was washed in. Sometimes I'd leave the paper under a lamp with gold-colored, peeling plastic.

One day, watching my mother clean is when I first got the idea of cards. I said, "Mama, I'm making you business cards."

"Do what now?" She had sprayed some ammonia on a window and turned her back to me. I watched her behind wiggle as she cleaned the window like she was rubbing a hole in it.

"I said I'm making you up some business cards so you can leave them around when you done."

"Girl, don't nobody want my business on a card," she said, turning to see what I was talking about. I had written a curly *R* and *A* for Ruby Arlington on my notebook paper in red ink. "Gone mess around and get me fired talking about some cards. This room is suppose to be *clean* when I leave it. When people pay for this room and come in, they see that it's clean. As clean a room as they ever gone get. That's my business card. Now keep your head in that book you brought and stop worrying me so I can finish and we can get home."

I had put the scraps away and started reading my American history book. But I was still thinking that my mother should get credit for her work. So I sometimes left scraps of paper, even though she told me not to. I thought she should be known and envisioned her becoming famous for her work, like maybe on the TV show "Real People."

When I started to my new school in the sixth grade, I bragged that my mama was the best motel room cleaner there was because I knew they'd be impressed and then I'd make a lot of friends.

"So what? Your mother's a maid," said one kid who was always trying to spit on the other kids and getting in trouble for it.

Lisa, this girl whose blonde hair was always greasy, and who usually smelled like pee, thought it was kind of interesting. So did Melvin, who I secretly loved. All his clothes were studded like a superstar's. Nobody liked Lisa, even though she was always trying to buy people, because she was trashy. Nobody liked Melvin because he was new, and nobody liked me because I was black and new. But after a while, I wasn't new anymore, and eventually they tolerated my blackness.

I was only eleven, and when I think back, when I remember, I can't believe how good-hearted I was, how young. I can't believe my mother was so young, just in her thirties, when she seemed so old to me.

I steal glances at my mother as I'm driving. She looks somber, not peaceful like she usually does. Her expression triggers a memory: I'm leaving for college, USC, on scholarship. It's two years after Owen, my brother, has moved out and already started his own family, one year before my father leaves my mother, and we're still a family. I'm crying because I'm afraid to leave home. I'm only seventeen, but I know that the next time I see her I'll be even more of a stranger. She'll be the same and I'll be different, and home won't be home. I can't say all this to her. I just say, "Mama," and hug her good-bye. She holds my face in her hands and says, "Ain't no need of crying. You going now."

I can never leave my mother's house quickly. I'm always in a hurry, and she's always keeping me with small talk and questions. This time she's asking about my trip to Tuscany that Max paid for, even though I'm sure she doesn't know where Tuscany is. Max wanted me to meet his family, see where he came from, but it could have been to Tuscany, Iowa, it wouldn't have made any difference. And Max, I don't even like to talk about him to my mother, who doesn't like him but tries not to show it. And Max, he doesn't *dislike* my mother, but neither has he ever said that he really liked her.

The first time she met Max was at a family gathering, my Aunt Ruthie's sixtieth birthday, which nobody who was alive and around could miss and show their faces ever again. Max and I were late, so when we walked through my Aunt Ruthie's door everybody was already drinking and dancing to Eddie Cleanhead Vinson singing *Homeboy, homeboy, looks like you drunk again.* Playing spades at one table and dominoes at another, talking trash at both.

Owen put his cards down long enough to rise and say, "Hey." All my female relatives thought Max was handsome, gathered around him and told him, "You so fine," which made him turn red, and my mother was shy and polite and quiet. So Max stuck with my brother and Uncle Ra Ra, who shoved a glass of brandy in his hand and immediately nicknamed him "Mass" before Massimo got to tell him he could call him Max. Owen slapped Max on the back and told me between brags and talking trash at the card table that any dude who had money and treated me right was all right with him.

Still, I worried all night, about who was thinking what about whom. What did Max think of all my loud drunk relatives? What did they all think of me for bringing in this, this Mass? *You know proper-talkin Avery would turn up with some white boy.* Later that night in bed with Max, in his own house which would become mine in a matter of weeks, he said that my mother was nice but kind of boring. I was angry, at the time, that he would call my mother boring, but I allowed myself to believe he didn't know how to say best in English what he actually meant, because he was Italian.

And so, I can still to this day be angry at Max about calling my mother boring, but I can never stay in her house long myself. I'm always antsy to leave it. I don't know if it's because I'm bored or because every time I'm in my mother's house, the house I grew up in, everything in it is a reminder, like the swap-meet prints of Jesus hanging everywhere, which my father would have never allowed when he was living here. I'm always begging her to stop buying all these tacky things and spend her money on things that she needs.

"Why don't you just cut it out, Mom?" I've said it forty times.

She used to have a couple of pictures of my father around, but those seem to be gone. He left her for another woman, and she's taken care of herself with little education while he started a new life. When my mother and father were together, they had terrible fights over money, other women, my mother's crazy, stubborn ways. There were loud voices, hitting, shoving. I wanted my mother to be quiet, stop arguing. She would never back down, not until my father left the house to get away from the fighting. I always blamed her for chasing Daddy away—for never shutting up, just once. But now that she's more like the woman I thought I wanted her to be, just a tiny bit more weak, I've figured out there are many different ways to be weak.

"Mom," I used to say, "it's not too late to go back to school." But I don't say that anymore. What good, I often wonder, did a degree in art do for me? Make me completely unemployable. All those motel rooms so that I could "create," throw paint on canvases, and give her nothing in return.

Now we are sitting at the glass dining room table fanning ourselves and drinking water. Even though I really do have to be going, I ask her if she wants to go back to get her food stamps today. I only ask because I can see the tiredness on her face and I know she'll say no.

"No. I'm not messing around with them anymore today. Tomorrow, if it cools down, I'm a get over there then."

"OK, Mom," I say. "I should get going, then."

"Wait." My mother goes to her refrigerator and pulls out three bunches of mustard greens. "For your dinner." She smiles. "And let me give you this ham hock." She puts all of it in two plastic grocery bags and holds them out to me.

Greens are my favorite, and these are a rich, lush green, like a neon crayon. They don't go with what I'm serving, though: four courses of food with pronunciation that never rolls off my tongue like it does Max's. Italian food. I tell my mother this.

"What kind of dinner don't go with greens?" She frowns. "I never heard tell of that before. You must be having Max's friends over. All them Euro-peeans."

"Mom," I say. "Please." But what she says is true.

I first met one of Max's best friends—Christian the Austrian, I call him—at a dinner party thick with Germans, Austrians, and Italians. Christian served roast duck for ten of us and told stories of his exploits in Naples. I'd never had duck before, and I thought it was greasy and fleshy. I preferred chicken.

"That's a bit south of Rome, Avery," he informed me about Naples parenthetically. I knew exactly where it was because I had been there.

"She knows where it is, you asshole," Max said. He drunkenly flicked ashes from his Dunhill on the white tablecloth. And later he yelled at me for not sticking up for myself. "I have seen you strong. When you want. But you fall into yourself around these, these *jokers*. You become a mouse. They intimate you. Why Avie?"

"*Intimidate*," I said sullenly. Max was right, but how did I explain that sometimes I felt as though I was in grade school, but older and still not wiser? He was furiously mixing tumeric, cumin, and chili pepper for a paste. "That is what I said. *Intimate*. They already think I am only with you for your ass and you are with me for my wallet."

"What do you care what people think?" I had asked another time, one of the biggest fights we've ever had. When we first met, I considered being a cleaning woman for a short time, set my own hours, have some flexibility—until I could find another job. Max is well-off and older and free with his money. I wanted to be free with mine, too. But I had a degree in one pocket and no money in the other.

Max, lying beside me in bed, threw up his hands in frustration. "What will people think, Avie? I can take care of you."

"I want to take care of myself," I said.

"Have some respect for yourself. Don't clean people's toilets. You were educated at a university. You are smarter than all the idiots I know. It's stupid, this idea. Look." He pointed at the large oil painting I had done a few years ago, inspired by friends. There were three women's torsos, in different shades of brown, dancing. Max loved the painting and insisted we hang it, even though I wasn't sure about it myself. "See that, Avie? You did that. It's beautiful. I am so proud." He took my hands and massaged them. "These hands are for painting, not toilets. Definitely not for cooking. No." He grinned at me, and I smiled at him, even though we had been fighting like cobras just minutes before. "So." He punched a pillow and turned over on his side, his back to me. "I won't let you do it."

I never did do it. But I've always meant to argue the point of respect with Max, exactly the *point* of the job. Maybe I should stick up for myself more, but he doesn't give me the chance. The words are always out of his mouth first. And anyway, since then, Max and I have let each other down so many times that we've lost what we used to have. It's turned out that they were all right, about the ass and the wallet.

But here I am now, still, rushing away from my mother to run to Max. "Avery, I want you to have these greens," my mother says, holding them out to me.

"You should spend your money on you, Mom. You shouldn't be throwing it away like this."

"Money spent on you was never thrown away. Now, here," she says. "I ain't going to tell you again." So I take them and offer her some cash until she can get her food stamps.

"That Max's money?"

"Mom, does it matter?"

"It's Max's money," she says, her arms crossed. I put it away.

She walks me to the door and stands at the top of the driveway as I go to my car. "I sure wish you could spend more time," she says.

"Next time," I call up to her. I drive off and can see her waving, getting smaller and smaller in my rearview mirror. I know she won't go into the house until I'm out of sight. When I realize I don't deserve this, it fills me with sorrow.

"**Farsumaura,** polenta with Bolognese meat sauce, and a salad with radicchieto leaves . . ." Max ticks off the courses, all his fingers splayed except the pinky tucked into his palm. He jerks his head back to subdue a blue-black strand of hair that has fallen into his eyes. "What am I forgetting?"

"La Zuppa di Ceci del Corsi," I recite dutifully. Max's best friend, who he loves like a brother, Silvio Corsi, the man who taught him how to cook in Rome, made up this soup of thick chickpeas, but we can never simply say, "Silvio's soup." I've tried. *Zuppa di!* . . . Max will prompt. *Di Ce-ci del Cor-si*, I'll finish in my most exaggerated Italian.

"Yes," Max says, grinning. "Good girl." He pats me on the ass, rubs it. When he's grinning like this, boyish and mischievous, touching me like he still wants only me, he seems kind. These moments remind me of all the times we've invested in each other, through deaths and the births of people in our families. I forget how mean and demanding he can be, but only lately so demanding because I don't feel like fighting. He likes to give orders, likes things to be done his way, insisted on dinner this evening when he knew I had to drive to the suburbs to help my mother, would maybe like to stay. But when he grins at me, the squint of his right eyes still charms me, and I can almost forget that he's fucking the hostess at the restaurant he chefs at. Two shades darker than me, she is, which is sometimes all it takes to catch Max's eye.

"So you take the polenta and the salad." Max's sharp blue eyes scan the ceiling. "I do the rest." He swats my ass for emphasis. "Is OK?"

I suppose. But either way, because Max isn't really expecting me to say no, I don't answer. He won't ever let me cook food he thinks is too complicated for me. Not in three years of living together. He even checks to see how I boil water.

"We don't have a vegetable," I say. I remember my mother's greens. I go to the refrigerator and pull them out. "We could cook these."

I'm picking a fight, that's all. Max planned the dinner a week ago and will not want to serve these with his other courses, I already know. Or maybe I'm not picking a fight. Maybe I'm giving him the chance to indulge me in the smallest thing, like when we first met and everything I said was endearing and every minute he told me I was beautiful.

"Avie, those don't go." He brushes past me and buries his head in the refrigerator. "There is spinaci," he says muffled, far away. He pulls his head out. Bottles clink and rattle when he slams the door. "A little olive oil and garlic. It will be fine."

"I think mustard greens will go just as well with polenta."

"Too heavy. Spinaci is better."

"You could let people decide, Massimo. We could cook *both*."

He stares at me with his hands on his waist. I don't even want the greens, not that badly. I just want the final word this time.

"You are whining like a kid."

"What's wrong with my mother's greens?" I still have them in my hands. I shake them at him.

"My head," Max mutters. "With them, nothing is wrong." He holds his head in his hands and massages his temples. "But you. You are another matter."

This dinner tonight will be a disaster, if not for Silvio. Pretty candles and nice presentation doesn't clear the air. Max's old friends and coworkers from his first restaurant—Lucky, Sanchez, and Sanchez's girlfriend—will come. "It has been too long," Max said when planning the dinner. Silvio will come, too, and I like him best of all Max's friends. He's warm. He's truly kind. He teases me, calls me Black Beauty.

"Black Beauty is a horse," I said, the first time he called me that.

"But, ah, Bellisima," he teased, "you are just as beautiful as the horse." He's the only one I want to talk to tonight.

Max is not speaking to me because I ruined the polenta. It should have been thick and firm enough to quiver when I shook it.

"What have you done to the polenta!" he yelled as if I had cut off his right arm. It was thin and runny as soup when I spooned it into one of our best serving bowls.

"Massimo," Silvio said gently, trying to smooth things. "It's only cornmeal. Right, Avery?" He kissed me on the forehead and I appreciated the scratchiness of his gray beard. He stuck his finger in the mess and tried not to make a face after he tasted it.

So we're getting by without it and Max looks at everyone but me. There are eight of us, and the rest are doing their best to pretend they're not uncomfortable because the hosts are not speaking to each other. It's the worst thing Max can do to me, ignore me, look through me. I'd rather he throw a plate across the room, which is what he usually does when he's most furious.

To cope, everybody's getting drunk from the several bottles of wine the guests have brought for dinner. Max sulks and chain-smokes. I pour wine like water and think about how I don't like Sanchez's date, Cookie, beautiful and caramel colored, dressed like a hooker. Fishnet stockings. I don't know who wears those anymore. They brought a friend, Theresa, who seems distant and snotty, probably because she's one of the most beautiful women I've ever seen, with hair for days and eyes the color of emeralds. Max somehow met her and thought I'd like her because she reminded him of me, which is mind-boggling. Because Sanchez, who *is* handsome, only seems to be interested in catching his reflection in the window and watching Theresa's every move, I like Lucky and Silvio the best tonight. They fight good-naturedly and are a study in opposites, enormous Lucky, near 300 pounds, and lanky Silvio. They keep my mind off of Max.

While Leonard Cohen sings in monotone from the CD player, Theresa decides to tell a story that she heard earlier, she says, about a parrot who was fed laxatives at the last party she went to. "And so this bird, it shits all over *everything*. I was *dy*ing! It was quite funny," she says. We all laugh politely and keep drinking, and Leonard Cohen gets more and more on my nerves. Max loves him for some reason, but I hate him; to me he sings like he's at a funeral that never ends. Parties aren't supposed to be reminiscent of funerals. I think about the last time I really had fun at a gathering, four years ago when my family first met Max. At the end of the night, Uncle Ra Ra said he was tired of me watching everybody else dance. He dragged me out into his living room to dance with him to the Ohio Players,

Roller coaster! Of love, say what? And then Max cut in on us and we danced close and slow, even though it was a fast song.

All day worrying and worrying about getting to where I needed to be and this is it. A dinner funeral.

"Jesus," Lucky says, finally tired of sparring with Silvio. "What the fuck?" He motions toward the stereo. "What are you trying to do? Depress us?"

I look around at all the people in our house. In Max's house. I want to be somewhere else. "That story? About the uh, the uh, bird?" I stutter. Theresa looks at me expectantly. I turn up a wine bottle and drink from it. I think I'm getting sick drunk. I can't tell yet. "That is the stupidest shit I ever heard."

Silvio's brought me outside to look at the stars because he thinks I need some air. "Silvio, I'm not so drunk that I don't know you can't see stars in L.A." I lean on him, wrap my arms around him. He's so tall that my face rests just below his chest.

"Yes, you can see them," he says. "Just squint like this." He takes off his tiny round silver glasses that make him look like he belongs in the 1920s. His eyes, syrupy brown, aren't as enormous without them. "Do the face like this." He crunches up his face and chuckles after he makes sure I imitate him. I do, but I still can't see anything.

"Ah, is OK. You can keep trying," he says, resting his head on top of my cropped, fuzzy head. I like that Silvio lets me lean into him. I like how his deep voice vibrates through his chest into my ear. He's warm and I feel so cold.

I rub his back, and he even lets me pull the shirttail from his pants, but this may only be because he's surprised. He doesn't stop me until my hands touch the bare skin on the small of his back, underneath the waist of his khakis.

"Bella, you are drunk. And I am old enough to be your father." He pulls my hand from his pants and traps it between his own large hands. Silvio looks at me as if I'm an amusing but incorrigible child.

And then I'm startled by Max's voice behind us. "Those things, yes," he says from a place in the yard I can't see. "And the third thing is that you are like a fucking father to *me*."

In the house, everyone puts on their jackets in a hurry and Silvio tries to calm Max down, but Max refuses. Silvio tries to pry my arms from around his waist, but I won't let go. I might fall down. "Massimo," he says, "we are all very drunk and tired, that is all. Avie meant nothing, no harm."

"Why are you speaking for her!" Max shouts after snatching a cigarette from his lips. He's failed to light it three times now. "Let me hear what she has got to say about it all."

Nothing. I have nothing to say. It's all I can do to make it to the bathroom to vomit.

Not until everyone leaves the house does Max smash half the dishes in the house and call me twenty different kinds of whores—in English and Italian.

"But what about the whore at the restaurant!" I've been saving this bombshell for maximum strength. He didn't know that I knew until now.

"That is different!" Max shoots back after a moment of shock. "She is not family!"

I'm much too drunk and much too sad and tired to argue that point, unlike my mother years and years ago.

We leave everything broken and I imagine that tomorrow Max will say this just isn't working anymore. And if he does, what will I do? I haven't had a job in three years, not since living with Max. How easily I was had. A tiramisu, compliments of Massimo the chef, and soon I was in his bed and living in his house, both of us stricken by the foreignness of the other. And how easily I had let Max down, faking a strength to match his, strength that's harder and harder to find.

I try to get to sleep on the couch in the living room, fighting waves of nausea and listening for sounds of Max tossing and turning in bed. It's so sad, how much he used to love me in that bed. How he used to marvel at the contrast between our skin. We used to lie side by side on our backs, my dark arm against his nearly translucent one, reaching toward the ceiling.

"How beautiful, Avie," he would say. "How beautiful is the skin." And I would laugh at his bad syntax that was so charming.

Everything's swervy and wavy and I just want to fall asleep. I barely know where I am. I might be dying. I truly think I might be dying. Mama help me, like when I was a child and you rubbed Vicks salve all over my body. Or when you rubbed away the cramps in my leg that hurt so badly I screamed myself to sleep.

If I weren't so ill, I'd get in my car and drive to you. Tomorrow? Maybe tomorrow. But if it were now, and if I knew where I was, I'd get on the 101 freeway, then take the 10 to the 60. I'd make a right and go down Montana, where my elementary, junior high, and high school are all in a row. At the four-way stop I'd make a left onto Arboles, where I used to play with Ashley in the seventh grade. I'd make another left on Verdugo, to your house, Mama, in the center of all the houses on the dead end. When I got to your house I'd ring the doorbell, even though I have a key. Maybe you'd be surprised to see me, stand in the doorway and forget to let me in. The happiness on your face would shame me. You'd say, "What?" Pull your nightgown tight across your chest. "Did you forget something? Is everything OK?"

"Mama," I'd say finally. "I'm lost."

acknowledgments

The story "Melvin in the Sixth Grade" was previously published in the *Missouri Review* and "Mouthful of Sorrow" in the *American Literary Review*.

I would like to thank my family and friends for their guidance and support, especially Lou Mathews, Tony Ardizzone, Alison Umminger, Mimi Lind, Sabrina Williams, Cathy Bowman, Laura Williams, Alyce Miller, Romayne Rubinas, Brian Ingram, Daryl Brown, Thomas Jones, Mark LaMonda, Mia Taylor, Ellie Partovi, Zohren Partovi, and Gerhard Taeubel, because you are always in my thoughts.

the flannery o'connor award
for short fiction